The Dragon's Surprise

Tahoe Dragon Mates
Book 7

Jessie Donovan

Mythical Lake Press, LLC

The Dragon's Surprise
Copyright © 2025 Laura Hoak-Kagey
Mythical Lake Press, LLC
Print Edition

Cover Art by Laura Hoak-Kagey of Mythical Lake Design
ISBN: 979-8891560758

Also by Jessie Donovan

Stonefire Dragons

Asylums for Magical Threats

Blaze of Secrets (AMT #1)

Frozen Desires (AMT #2)

Shadow of Temptation (AMT #3)

Flare of Promise (AMT #4)

Cascade Shifters

Convincing the Cougar (CS #0.5)

Reclaiming the Wolf (CS #1)

Cougar's First Christmas (CS #2)

Resisting the Cougar (CS #3)

Love in Scotland

Crazy Scottish Love (LiS #1)

Chaotic Scottish Wedding (LiS #2)

WRITING AS KAYLA CHASE

(Steamy small-town contemporary romance)

Starry Hills

Want Me Forever

Stay With Me Forever

Marry Me Forever

Trust Me Forever

Chapter One

Alexis "Lexi" Sakamoto parked her car in front of a two-story building on a mountain in the Greater Lake Tahoe area, shut off the ignition, and took a deep breath. *Remember, don't yell at the dragonman as soon as you see him. That won't help anyone, but especially not the boy.*

"Lexi?"

She turned around until she could look at the child in the backseat. His big, green eyes were uncertain, and almost afraid.

Not that she could blame him. Ethan Jones had been abandoned by his mother two weeks ago, left at the dragon orphanage as soon as she'd given up any parental rights.

Apparently, she'd believed the child to be her husband's and not the one-night stand she'd had during a short breakup seven years ago.

The one she'd had with a dragon-shifter.

As the young boy's pupils flashed between round and slitted, he closed his eyes and held his head. "He's so loud, Lexi. Tell him to stop."

Her heart clenched at his confusion and pain. His inner dragon speaking to him for the first time—a kind of second personality inside his head—right before his mother had abandoned him probably only reminded Ethan of why he was visiting a dragon-shifter clan today.

Lexi had no idea how his mother had been able to give him up since Ethan was an amazing little boy. However, cursing his mother would do nothing, so Lexi reached back to pat his leg and said, "I know he's loud, Ethan. But the people here understand you and can help you learn how to talk with your dragon. And just wait. I bet you and your inner dragon will be best friends before you know it."

He let go of his head, his pupils staying round, and frowned. "But Mommy said I need to ignore him and make him go away. Or, at least..."

He trailed off and stared out the window as he fidgeted with his seat belt. Lexi's heart ached, knowing firsthand what it was like to be abandoned by a mother at a young age and to constantly wonder what you'd done wrong.

No. The boy had done nothing wrong. He was half dragon-shifter, and since the gene was always dominant, he'd had no choice in the matter.

And while the father had never known of his existence, she'd never heard back from any of the emails or messages she'd left. And usually if the Dragon Orphan Care System—or DOCS—left a message, most dragon-shifters would return the call or email.

However, not Dr. Kyle Baker.

Focusing on Ethan, she asked, "Are you finally ready to meet a dragon-shifter?"

He looked down, swinging his feet. "I guess."

By all accounts, when Ethan had first been left at the orphanage, he'd thought his mother would be right back. He'd been friendly, cheerful, and interested in painting or coloring or anything artistic.

But as it sunk in that his mother wasn't coming back, Lexi had tried her best to keep his spirits up. She wished she could take him home, give him some love, and help him adjust.

However, the inner dragon half started talking to their human halves around ages five or six. And without guidance, it could spell disaster later on with a rogue dragon, one that didn't listen and could end up getting the dragon-shifter killed.

So she'd had no choice but to come here, to Clan MirrorPeak, and hope Ethan's biological father would help him. Or if not him specifically, at least the clan as a whole, since all the long-term DOCS facilities were full.

Okay, time to finally meet with Ethan's father and see why he's been ignoring me. Lexi grabbed her purse, exited the car, and went around to take Ethan out of his booster seat. As soon as she shut the door, he took her hand. Lexi squeezed his fingers and smiled down at him. "Come on. Like I said, I'll be here for at least a few weeks. I'm going to make sure you're happy and settled before I leave. Okay?"

He bobbed his head even as his eyes were wary.

She wanted to hug the little boy, and yet, part of her job was to avoid getting overly attached.

Reminding herself that she couldn't give every dragon-shifter orphan a home and that her job helped so many, she gently tugged Ethan's hand and entered Clan MirrorPeak's main security building.

Dr. Kyle Baker finished the last of his paperwork for the day and stretched his arms above his head.

His inner dragon spoke up. *Does this mean we can go flying for a bit? It's been days.*

Sorry, dragon. After this morning, I'm too tired.

Eli is doing well, though.

He'll live, yes. But the rest is going to take time...

His beast huffed. *That's in the future, though. A small break away from the clan, in the air, will do us good.*

Our job isn't to abandon patients for personal time.

It's not just personal, it's essential. You barely act like a dragon-shifter most days.

Before he could argue back, there was a knock on his office door and the face of his boyhood friend, Daniel

Torres, appeared. He entered, shut the door, crossed his arms over his chest, and studied him with his dark brown eyes. Something was up.

Kyle raised an eyebrow. "What now?"

"Did you receive anything from DOCS?"

"The dragon orphan system? No, why should I? No one's adopted recently, have they?"

Daniel nodded toward his computer. "Check. Now."

Kyle may have been friends with Daniel when they were younger, but the male was now a Protector and part of clan security. And while Kyle wanted to ask what the hell he was talking about, he opened his email and did a search. Four emails came up from a female named Lexi Sakamoto, the titles getting more over-the-top as they went:

Please respond immediately

This is urgent and needs your attention

Ignoring me again will result in consequences

Last warning before I show up at your doorstep unannounced

He clicked the last email and scanned the contents:

Dr. Baker,

As discussed previously, a young boy was tested, and

the DNA proves he's your son. Since you've ignored all of my emails, as well as messages I left at your clinic's front desk, I will show up on Clan MirrorPeak at the time and date below. I'll stay for two or three weeks, and we'll discuss more when we get there. Evade me again and the American Department of Dragon Affairs will get involved.

He blinked, ignoring the rest. "Son?"

Daniel snorted. "Caught that part, did you?"

His gaze shot to Daniel's. "What the fuck is she talking about?"

"You're the one who has one-night stands with human females every six months or so. And given how you love percentages, you should know no form of birth control is 100 percent effective, apart from abstinence."

He stood and growled. "It's been over a year since my last encounter. And I'm always careful."

"That may be, but I've seen the boy, and there's no doubt he's yours, Kyle." His voice softened. "His mother abandoned him as soon as his inner dragon started talking to him."

"But that means..."

"Yes, he's six years old."

He tried to remember back seven years, but all he recalled was a hazy female with blonde hair.

She would've told him she was pregnant and kept the child. Wouldn't she have?

His inner beast spoke up. *DNA doesn't lie. Let's at least meet him.*

Ignoring his dragon, he looked back at Daniel. "Surely someone else can look after him. I'll provide anything he needs when it comes to clothes or food or the like. But I don't have time to look after a child."

"Rio already said you were coming to meet him."

Rio Alvaro was their clan leader, and the only person who outranked Kyle inside MirrorPeak, which meant he had no choice.

His inner dragon spoke up. *Stop dragging your feet. If this boy is with DOCS, it means his mother gave him up. He's probably scared.*

I don't doubt that. But I don't have time to raise him. It'd be unfair to the boy, as well as to our patients.

When will you stop letting what happened in our first year as a doctor rule your life?

Not wanting to talk about how his foolishness had nearly killed someone, Kyle discarded his white lab coat and replied to Daniel, "Fine, I'll go and speak with Miss Sakamoto about his care. I'm sure we can find a solution."

Daniel, who had mated a human and was expecting his first child soon, narrowed his eyes. "He's a little boy, lost and alone, not a book you can hand off to someone else."

"I'm the only doctor here, Daniel. I can't afford to be distracted or take time off to settle him in since I have to look after the entire clan. And after what I had to do this morning to save Eli, I'd think you'd understand my priorities."

Before the dragonman could utter a reply, Kyle walked past Daniel, toward the clinic's exit. He'd make sure the boy had everything he needed and then find a solution that worked for everyone. That was the only way he could protect his clan while also working toward redemption for the mistake he'd made when he'd been young and selfish.

Chapter Two

Lexi watched Ethan as he colored the dragon picture with some crayons. A heavily pregnant human named Jenny Torres filled in another picture next to him, chatting about everything and nothing. Ethan seemed to relax around her, which was good seeing as Lexi would have to leave Ethan with Jenny when she went to meet with Kyle Baker alone. At least now, she wouldn't have to worry about Ethan being scared.

Jenny smiled at her and said, "You haven't been to MirrorPeak for as long as I've lived here, which is about seven months. Are the other clans the same with how they're set up and run? I want to visit them all someday, but Daniel says not yet. Something about the clans wanting to make alliances, but ADDA is making it difficult." She bit her lip and sighed. "I wasn't supposed to say that. I mean, you're sort of tied to ADDA, aren't you?"

ADDA was what most people called the American Department of Dragon Affairs, the agency that ruled over all dragon-shifters in the US. "Yes and no. Although my older sister, Jennifer Sakamoto, works for them formally."

"Well, she has the best name, so she must be a good person."

Jenny grinned, and Lexi couldn't help but smile. Something about the woman made her feel as if she'd known her forever and hadn't just met her. "We argued like all sisters do, but I love her, and she really tries to help the dragon-shifters. She's friends with Ashley Swift."

Jenny's eyes widened. "I know Ashley! I'll have to see if she'll bring your sister around. The more good and dedicated ADDA employees I know, the better, I think. Especially as I'll need them on my side if I'm to write my dragon textbooks for human children."

Lexi was about to ask for more information when Jenny's mate, Daniel, knocked and entered the room. He gave a loving look at Jenny, and Lexi tried to ignore the twinge of jealousy that shot through her. Like a lot of girls, she'd dreamed of living with the dragons and finding her own dragonman as a kid. However, after years of dealing with unwanted children from dalliances between the dragonmen and human women, she'd become rather cynical.

Daniel looked at her and said, "Come on. I'll take you to him."

Standing, Lexi asked Ethan, "Will you be okay here with Miss Jenny?"

He glanced down at his crayons, and before he could answer, Lexi added, "I'll be back, I promise. And I've never broken one yet, have I?"

He shook his head.

Jenny reached over, put an arm around his shoulders, and hugged him to her side. "We'll have tons of fun, Ethan. I have paints and colored paper and all kinds of things. I used to be an elementary school teacher, so no one can craft like me."

He glanced at Jenny. "Okay."

Lexi wanted to hug the boy. And yet, as Daniel motioned for them to go, securing Ethan's future was more important. "Have fun, Ethan. I'll be back soon."

She followed the tall dragonman down the hallway until he stopped and gestured at a closed door. "Kyle's inside. Go in whenever you're ready."

After taking a deep breath, she nodded. "I'm ready."

Lexi turned the knob, entered, and stopped as she crashed into something hard and stumbled. Hands gripped her shoulder to keep her from falling, and she looked up. Green eyes, the exact shade of Ethan's, stared down at her, pupils flashing between round and slitted. He had long, brown hair pulled back from his face, pale skin, and a slightly too-long nose. Not that it detracted from his strong jaw or firm lips, or pretty eyes.

He grunted, released her, and Lexi stumbled until she could stand on her own two legs. The man spoke up. "Alexis Sakamoto, I presume?"

His calm, almost impatient tone snapped her back to reality, reminding her of how he'd ignored both her and the poor boy in the room down the hall. "Yes. And you, Dr. Baker, are in some trouble."

Kyle didn't like to sit still if he could help it, so he'd paced around the small room, wondering what was taking so long when the door opened and someone barreled into him. He stopped her from falling and was about to tell her to be careful when she looked up at him.

He couldn't look away from her dark brown eyes. She had light tan skin, short black hair, and was quite possibly the most beautiful female he'd ever seen.

Then his dragon spoke up. *If this is the DOCS employee, then she can scold us all she wants.*

Don't start.

Why not? She's pretty, and definitely has some backbone, if her emails are anything to go by. And you need that.

Alarm bells rang inside his head, and Kyle released the female quickly. She stumbled slightly, but regained her balance. He forced his voice to be calm and detached as he asked, "Alexis Sakamoto, I presume?"

Her dazed look faded away, replaced with a scowl. "Yes. And you, Dr. Baker, are in some trouble."

His dragon laughed, but Kyle ignored him. "As I'm sure you know, I didn't know about the child's existence. So what am I in trouble for?"

"Ignoring me for two weeks. Two weeks where that boy has been alone and scared and trying to understand what to do with his inner dragon. It's all new to him, and frightening. I've done what I could, but I'm not a dragon-shifter." She walked over and poked him in the chest. "You need to help him. And quickly."

Ignoring the heat that flared at her touch, he narrowed his eyes. "My clan will help him, of course. But I only found out that this boy existed half an hour ago. Give me a little grace."

"Why? You're the one who slept with a human, knew this could happen, and now you have to be the adult and face the consequences."

"I am an adult, one responsible for the health of the entire clan. Are you saying they don't matter?"

"Of course I'm not saying that! But as soon as you put your dick into someone, you were possibly signing up for this."

She gasped and slapped a hand over her mouth, clearly mortified.

On a better day, maybe when he hadn't just found out he had a son, or hadn't nearly lost a patient in the morning, he would've been more diplomatic.

But his usual restraint snapped, and he moved

closer, lowering his head toward her. "So you've been celibate your whole life, then? Or were you embracing possible motherhood every time someone fucked you?"

As soon as the words left his mouth, Kyle regretted it. What the hell was wrong with him?

His dragon spoke up. *She knows how to break your carefully constructed walls. Good.*

Stepping back, he murmured, "I'm sorry. That was uncalled for."

She crossed her arms over her chest and nodded. "It was." She unfolded her arms. "But I was also out of line, so I'm sorry. It's just been tough because Ethan is kind and curious and is constantly wondering why his mother left him. And as someone who was abandoned at an early age—when my mother left my sister and I at our grandmother's house one night, never to return—it's become rather personal. More so than the ones who are surrendered as babies, with no memory of their birth moms."

At the vulnerable look in her eyes, Kyle wondered if she'd planned to share that much. But at least her overreaction and anger made a lot more sense now. After taking a deep breath, he asked, "Shall we start over? I'll help with what I can, but I also want what's best for the boy. As the sole doctor here, I'm not sure me taking him in and raising him is it. Even now, I barely have enough time to sleep."

Tilting her head, she studied him a few beats before replying, "I get that, but please, at least meet him. I didn't tell Ethan that his father is here, just that he'd stay with MirrorPeak and learn how to handle his inner dragon from other dragon-shifters."

"You didn't tell him about me?"

She rolled her eyes. "Of course not. I wouldn't get his hopes up like that. This is far from my first rodeo, Dr. Baker."

His dragon spoke up. *Just meet the boy. We need to help him, if nothing else. Because if he can't handle his inner dragon, it won't end well.*

You know I don't teach the young ones how to handle their inner beasts.

Maybe not, but we all went through it. Besides, you'll need to examine him and run tests soon, to make sure he's healthy since the human doctors might've missed something. The less anxious he is around you, the better.

I know what you're doing. But don't expect anything, dragon, because I don't have time for anything but being a doctor.

His beast sniffed. *I didn't say anything.*

Resisting a sigh, Kyle replied to the human, "Fine. But don't share that I'm his father because I'm not. Not in any of the ways it matters."

"Very well. But one last thing before I take you to Ethan—I'm staying with your clan for at least two weeks, to ensure Ethan transitions well into MirrorPeak's care, and I'll be watching you."

His dragon spoke up. *Good. I like her. Maybe we can rile her some more. That was fun.*

Behave, dragon.

Why? You never go anywhere, see anyone, or do anything. So I take what I can get.

Ignoring his beast, he opened the door and motioned. "Understood, Ms. Sakamoto. Now, come on. I've been awake a long time and I need to go home and rest before another emergency crops up."

Then he walked out without a backward glance.

Lexi was still berating herself for being unprofessional when Kyle strode out of the room and she struggled to keep up.

Why, oh why, had she told him about her mom leaving her and Jennifer? Her sister would no doubt chew her out for that later, as Jennifer liked to keep her private life private.

Thankfully, the walk was short, and she quickly met up with the dragonman who stood waiting for her at the door. She glanced up, willing herself not to notice his remarkable eyes again, and said softly, "Be nice to him. He's gone through a lot lately."

His expression softened as his pupils flashed. "I'm a doctor, Ms. Sakamoto. I would never deliberately hurt anyone."

"Lexi."

He frowned. "What?"

There she went, being unprofessional again, but it was too late to take it back. "You can call me Lexi."

He nodded, but said nothing else, so Lexi opened the door and walked in. She smiled as Ethan met her gaze, then he looked at Kyle and she noticed his whole body stiffened. His actions made Lexi wonder what his so-called father back in his old home had done to him once he'd found out the truth. Because in her experience, Ethan always did better with women than men.

Doing her best to hide her concerns, she walked over to Ethan, placed a hand on his shoulder, and gestured toward Kyle. "This is Dr. Kyle Baker, the dragon doctor here."

Ethan moved to lean against her. "Is he going to poke me?"

Kyle stared at Ethan, his pupils flashing, and Lexi wished she knew what he was thinking.

Please let him be nicer to Ethan. Please.

The dragonman finally cleared his throat and said, "I won't poke you unless it's necessary, I promise. I hated needles as a kid, so I try to avoid them, if possible."

Ethan frowned. "But you're a doctor. Doctors can't be afraid of needles."

Kyle almost smiled, and Lexi did her best not to notice how much more handsome the dragonman was when he wasn't frowning. The doctor said, "Just because we're afraid of something when we're a kid doesn't mean we can't learn to be strong and overcome it."

The boy's reply was barely audible as he whispered, "I'm afraid of my dragon. Can you help with him?"

The doctor's pupils flashed rapidly, and she glanced down at Ethan, who watched Kyle closely, with fascination.

An awkward silence fell—one that Lexi could murder the doctor for, as any sort of encouragement would've helped Ethan—until Jenny spoke up. "We'll all help you, Ethan. And I, for one, have had enough talk about needles and would rather do something more fun. And since Ethan said he's never seen a dragon up close, I thought we could go to the second landing area and Kyle could show him his."

For a beat, Lexi wondered if the dragon doctor would run. He definitely looked like he wanted to. But she waited, knowing this would be an important first step in learning if the dragonman would eventually accept his son or not. Her hopes weren't high, but she wanted nothing more than to be wrong.

Kyle was still trying to get his head around the small boy who looked so much like him, to the point he didn't need DNA results to tell him the child was his. He had the same eyes and nose, and looked like every baby picture his aunt still showed him, albeit Ethan's hair was blonder than Kyle's had been before turning brown.

For a split second, he'd felt regret. Dragon-shifters

treasured children, especially given their lower birth rates. At least, they'd been lower until recent years with advancements in medicine.

But then he reminded himself he hadn't known, and he couldn't change the past.

Then Jenny had to go and suggest Kyle showing his dragon to the boy, which snapped him back to the present. He frowned at the female. "Why me?"

Jenny stared at him and raised her eyebrows. "Because neither Lexi nor I can do it, and you're here. And don't suggest Daniel, since he's about to do some patrols."

There were others who could've done it instead. And yet, as Jenny continued to stare at him in a way that would make any student squirm in their seats, he mentally sighed. Well, the female did have more experience with kids than him, so he'd take her lead. For now.

He cleared his throat. "All right. Now is best since, barring any emergency, I shouldn't be needed at the clinic for a while."

Ethan frowned at him. "You talk weird."

Both females bit their lips to keep from laughing, but Kyle focused on the boy. "Er, sorry. I don't have any brothers or sisters and haven't been around kids for a long time, unless they're sick."

Ethan tilted his head. "I don't have any brothers and sisters. I think." He glanced down and pushed one crayon around on the desk. "I don't know my dad. My real dad. My dad, well, not really my dad, he said…"

The boy looked sad and lonely, and utterly miserable, and it wrenched Kyle's heart.

His beast spoke up. *Show him me, and it'll cheer him up.*

Kyle leaned down a little, bracing his hands on his thighs, and waited until Ethan met his eyes. "There are plenty of kids your age here, and you'll meet them soon. But for now, do you want to see a dragon up close?"

The boy nodded.

Straightening, Kyle met Lexi's eyes again. For a second, he swore approval flashed there, but it was gone before he could blink. "Then if it's okay with you, shall we go?"

Lexi glanced at Jenny. "If you don't mind? I know you're supposed to show me and Ethan to our temporary place, but..."

Jenny waved a hand in dismissal. "I don't mind a detour. Walking usually keeps my baby happy and makes them stop doing somersaults in my belly. Although, truth be told, I feel more like a penguin since I waddle more than walk. But that's okay, because I make a pretty cute penguin."

She winked, and Lexi smiled uncertainly. Kyle nearly chuckled. Jenny Torres was a kind female, loved her mate, and helped with the school. However, she was a little eccentric, and it took time to get used to her chatter.

Although Ethan didn't seem to mind it. He took

Jenny's hand. "I like penguins. But you're too big to be a penguin."

Jenny tapped her chin. "Maybe that's true. You'll have to help me think of a better animal on the way."

Kyle took that as his cue, so he opened the door and followed the females and the boy.

Jenny's ramblings allowed him to study Ethan, wondering what to do with him. Maybe Jenny and Daniel would adopt him.

His inner dragon sniffed and spoke up. *I still think we should at least get to know him and see if we can make it work. And don't say we wouldn't have time. Aunt Rita would help.*

He nearly groaned as he remembered his aunt. She'd want to see the boy, to spoil him, and would probably try her best to convince Kyle that he should raise him.

His inner dragon spoke again. *Aunt Rita is our only family. So finding out she has a great-nephew will make her happy.*

His aunt's only child had died at the age of ten from a then-untreatable form of dragon deteriorating syndrome—a disease that slowly attacked the dragon half until it died, before eating away at the brain. A cure was close, so very close. But that didn't help his aunt or Kyle's late cousin.

And after Kyle's parents had died from a trap laid by the League—the shorthand used for the America for Humans Only League, who believed the US should be purged of all dragon-shifters—he'd lived with his aunt, and she was like a second mother to him.

His beast added, *Just stop thinking of ways to foist Ethan on someone else. At least for now. He just needs to know he belongs on MirrorPeak.*

His dragon was right. Kyle was being selfish, thinking of his own future and neglecting the boy's. He would ultimately do what was best for Ethan, but he could at least help the boy settle in. *One of the first things Ethan needs to do is get used to dragons. So let's show him one.*

And maybe even let him slide down our side. That'll be fun.

They reached the smaller landing area, and Kyle waited for Jenny to turn them all around before he stripped his clothes. Then he stood, imagined his nose elongating into a snout, wings sprouting from his back, and his arms and legs growing into limbs. Once he stood in his gold dragon form, he grunted and waited to see how both Ethan and Lexi reacted.

Not that he should care about the human female. And yet, both man and beast wanted to impress her for reasons he didn't dare think about.

Chapter Three

L exi tried not to think about how Kyle Baker would be naked soon, as he changed from human to dragon. She most definitely didn't try to imagine what his shoulders might look like, let alone the rest of him.

Although his probably muscled body—given what she knew of dragon-shifters—wasn't the only reason. She'd never seen a dragon-shifter actually change forms in person before. Going from a six-foot-something human to a fifteen or twenty-foot dragon was magical and yet had to be a little uncomfortable. Not that any dragon-shifter had discussed that kind of thing with her. She tried her best to get to know the people adopting the orphan children, and yet she'd always been kept apart. Not just because she was human, but also because she tangentially worked for ADDA.

A loud grunt brought her back to the present. Jenny

motioned for them to turn around, and as soon as she saw the golden dragon glinting in the sun, her jaw dropped.

Of course he was a gold dragon. The sunshine made him look like some sort of living statue, his scales almost flashing like glitter in parts. His eyes, though, were serious like before, if a lot bigger with slitted pupils. As he glanced at her and then Ethan, uncertainty flashed. Was the gorgeous dragonman insecure? That seemed impossible.

Ethan stared and tugged at her hand. *The boy.* That's right, she needed to stop acting like a dragon-obsessed teenager and focus on Ethan. So she asked, "What do you think?"

He never took his gaze from Kyle's dragon form as he replied, "He's really big."

Jenny chimed in. "He's about average for a male dragon." The dragon grunted, and Jenny laughed. "Okay, a little bigger. How about we go up and pet him?"

Lexi frowned. "Pet him?"

Jenny bobbed her head. "Dragons love having their scales stroked. However, if you really want a dragon to become putty in your hands, then you scratch one behind their ear and they kind of purr."

She looked skeptically at Kyle's dragon. "Like a cat?"

"Yep. They're more like cats than you'd think. Difficult to win over at first, but once you do, you have a loyal friend or mate for life." Jenny held Ethan's other hand and tugged gently. "Come on. I'll show you what to do."

Lexi and Ethan followed Jenny's lead until they stood in front of Kyle's lowered head. The scales were even more beautiful in person, although the brief glimpse of giant teeth reminded her that if it came to it, a dragon would always win over a human.

Jenny reached out and patted Kyle's snout. "Try it. The scales are really smooth but warm, and not at all cold or metallic like they look. There's nothing like curling up against my mate's side when it's cold, in either form, and getting nice and toasty."

Kyle moved his head closer, until it was just in front of Ethan. He slowly released Lexi's hand to touch the snout. The boy laid his hand on the scales and rubbed back and forth. "They are warm and smooth!"

Lexi smiled and decided to find out for herself— because, really, when would she have this chance again? —before placing her hand at the side of his snout, just behind his nostril. As she stroked, she met the large dragon eye in front of her, and the pupil dilated a little. Did that mean the two halves were talking?

Then a rumbling sound made her jump, and Jenny laughed. "That means he likes it. Even buttoned-up, serious Kyle likes his dragon form pampered. If he lowers his head, I can show you how to really make him happy and be even louder."

Ethan nodded. "Yes! I want to hear him purr louder."

The dragon huffed, and Lexi smiled. "It's not quite a purr, Ethan. It's more like a cross between a purr and a growl, but more charming."

Jenny laughed. "I like that description. I may have to use it, since I've been trying to think of the best way to describe it."

Kyle's dragon lowered his head further, and Jenny snorted. "His dragon is impatient and wants pets." She motioned to behind the ear. "See that small patch of skin without scales? That's the spot. Try it."

Ethan looked at her, and Lexi nodded. "You go first."

The boy gingerly scratched the strip of skin, and a louder rumble came from the dragon's chest, and Ethan laughed. "He really is like a cat and purrs!"

The dragon huffed, and Lexi whispered, "Let's see how he does with both of us at the same time."

She moved to the other ear and scratched her nails at the tough but warm skin. The sound grew even louder, and she grinned before looking into the eye closest to her. She wasn't good at reading a dragon's body language, but she swore there was humor dancing there.

After about a minute, Kyle lifted his head, and Ethan cried out in protest. But the dragon tapped his tail against his side, and Jenny interpreted for them. "He'll let you slide down his side, if you want to. I think you should, since sliding down a dragon is one of the best things ever. And don't worry, he won't let you fall or get hurt."

Ethan looked up, up, up, and whispered, "But he's so

tall." He looked at Lexi. "Will you go first and show me?"

She resisted blinking. "Me?"

Jenny spoke up. "I'd do it, if I wasn't pregnant. But my coordination isn't the best when I'm not carrying a dragon baby, so I really can't do it when I'm this big. I promise it's safe, Lexi. I did it all the time when I first mated Daniel."

As Lexi eyed the height, Ethan tugged her hand. "If you're scared, it's okay. Because I'm a little scared too."

She glanced down just as Ethan's pupils flashed, and he shut his eyes. She kneeled down, and when he opened them again, his pupils were round. "Are you okay?"

"He's just loud. And wants to have fun."

Ethan's uncertain gaze went to the dragon's side again, which decided it. "Then let me try it first, so you can see that it's safe. Because I think that will make your dragon happy, won't it?"

"I think so."

"Okay." She stood. "So what do I do, Jenny?"

"He'll pick you up with his tail, put you on his back, and then you slide down when you're ready."

As Jenny spoke, Kyle laid down with his rear limbs under him and his front ones out straight in front of his body, with his tail moving back and forth. Lexi blurted, "He really does look like a cat."

The dragon nearly glared, but Lexi ignored the look, took a deep breath, and walked over, closer to his tail.

Kyle had never really had anyone touch his dragon form since he was a teenager, back when he and his friends had made stupid dares, ones that could've killed each other.

However, as first Ethan and then Lexi caressed his snout before scratching behind his ears, tension faded from his body, relaxing him in a way he hadn't experienced for years. Probably not since he'd become a fully-fledged doctor.

His dragon spoke up. *They could become our family.*

What are you talking about?

He's our son, just as lost as us. And she should be ours.

Not wanting to think too hard about what his dragon was saying, he was glad when Lexi finally walked up to him and said, "Okay, Mr. Dragon, be nice. I'm not the best with unstable heights, but I'm willing to try. However, if you drop me, I won't be responsible for my actions."

Kyle wanted to smile. If this female wasn't intimidated by his dragon form, she probably wasn't afraid of much.

His dragon said, *She's strong, yes, but also vulnerable, remember?*

Not wanting to dwell on the hurt look in her eyes from when she'd shared about her mother, he wrapped his tail around her middle and bobbed his head. After waiting a beat, just to make sure she didn't want to back out, he lifted her gently. She sucked in a breath, but he placed her in a sitting position on his back, keeping a hold of her until she seemed steady. Then he slowly unfurled his tail and moved it away.

She froze for a few beats before stroking his scales. His beast hummed, and Lexi smiled at him. She really was beautiful when she smiled.

His beast mentally laughed. *You'll want her like I do soon enough.*

Lexi said, "Okay, it looks pretty steep. Won't I fall off?"

Kyle's dragon moved out his hind leg, to create a gentler slope.

The female took a few deep breaths before she nodded. "I can do this." She glanced at him. "Don't you dare let me fall."

He shook his head.

She hesitated, and then slid down his flank and leg, until her feet reached the ground and he steadied her with his tail.

Lexi grinned at him. "That was actually pretty fun."

His beast spoke up. *She could have a lot of fun with us, in our human form, too.*

Don't start.

I want to see how long you can resist her.

Ethan's voice stopped him from replying to his beast. "Can I try, Dr. Baker? Please? Then maybe he'll stop demanding things in my head."

His dragon swung their head around, and at the boy's expression—a mixture of uncertainty and distress —both man and beast softened. Kyle sometimes forgot how confusing it could be when a dragon-shifter's inner dragon started talking to them.

His beast spoke up. *Let's help him.*

We'll see, dragon. We'll see.

Kyle bobbed his head and extended his tail before motioning for Ethan to come. And for the next little while, he focused on making the little boy smile.

Lexi watched as Kyle set his son on his back and helped him slide down his leg. She wished this were enough, and that by Kyle seeing his son happy, it meant everything would turn out well and he'd want to take care of Ethan.

However, in her experience, dragon-shifters who found out they suddenly had a child didn't always take it well. Especially since having a half-human kid meant greater scrutiny from the American Department of Dragon Affairs.

But even though it was far from easy, Lexi always kept trying to find the children families, even if it was with a new, adoptive family and not with their birth parent.

Unlike a lot of other people, she'd gone into this job with her eyes wide open. Her sister was a few years older, and so Lexi had been in high school when she'd first learned about the dragon orphan side of things and had volunteered. Even though she'd thought about joining ADDA, there were never enough people helping with DOCS, especially since the pay was worse.

However, as a kid who had been abandoned herself, she didn't care if she made a little less money. Every child who was formally adopted and found a forever home was something she couldn't put a price on.

And as she watched Ethan have another turn, she wished she had a better read on Kyle Baker. Even in his human form, she'd had trouble pinning him down and usually she was a good judge of character. At least when it came to how people viewed and treated children.

Jenny's voice interrupted her thoughts. "This is the most relaxed I've seen Kyle since I arrived."

She looked at the other woman, pouncing on the chance to find out more about the dragon doctor. "So he's usually the buttoned up, grumpy fellow from earlier?"

"Not always grumpy. But to be fair, he had a difficult surgery earlier today. One of the Protectors got injured by some human assholes, and he almost couldn't save him."

"But he did?"

Jenny bobbed her head. "Yes. He's an amazing doctor, especially with surgeries. Although, given his past..."

The other woman clamped her jaw tight, and Lexi asked, "What about his past?"

"No, I shouldn't have mentioned it. You'll have to ask him. But I think he likes you, so getting him to talk shouldn't be that hard."

She barked out a laugh. "Likes me? Why in the world would you say that? He's been nothing but dismissive since I arrived."

"He let you slide down his dragon."

"But that was just to help Ethan."

Jenny shrugged. "If you say so. Although here comes the boy."

Ethan skidded to a halt in front of them, his eyes bright with happiness. "That was really fun! Maybe I can do it again later? I only went three times. But my dragon liked it. He hummed for the first time in my mind!"

Lexi smiled at him. "I'm glad. And as soon as we settle in, we have an appointment at the school, and they should be able to help you get along even more. And don't worry, everyone will be gone by then, so you don't have to face the other kids just yet. However, I thought you might want to meet your teachers."

Ethan's happiness faded a little. "But I don't know anything about being a dragon-shifter. The other kids will make fun of me."

He glanced down, and Lexi squatted and stayed down until he finally met her eyes. "They'll teach you things slowly, okay? And you're the second older kid who's become a part of Clan MirrorPeak in the last few years, so the teachers know what to do. It'll be all right, I promise." He still didn't say anything, so she added, "I'm human, and learned a lot about dragon-shifters over the years, but not all. Maybe I can sit with you for the first private lesson, where it's just you, me, and the teacher? That way, we can learn together."

Ethan bobbed his head. "That sounds good."

She stood and took Ethan's hand. "Now, should we go and see where we're staying? It's supposed to be near a playground, one we can check out later, if you like?"

"I like swings, if they have some."

Jenny spoke up. "Yep, there are swings, and even a tire swing. I like the tire swing myself. Well, when I'm not pregnant. And I can bring my niece to come play too, as she's about the same age and really nice and friendly. She's the daughter of my mate's brother, if that makes sense?"

Ethan frowned. "Not really."

Jenny snorted. "Well, all you need to know is that she likes the swings, too. You could even have a competition to see who goes higher. Well, as long as you don't go too high. But you know what I mean. Do you want to meet her later?"

"Okay," Ethan said softly.

Jenny took Ethan's other hand. "Well, then let's get a move on. You still have a lot to do before you can play, and I definitely need a nap."

As Jenny kept chatting to Ethan, they walked away

from the landing area. However, Lexi looked over her shoulder to see Kyle's dragon watching them. And once he finally disappeared from sight, hidden behind the wall surrounding the landing area, she pushed aside regrets at not getting to see him shift back into his human form.

Although she refused to think too much about why she was disappointed.

Chapter Four

Kyle knew he should stop by the clinic and check on things instead of heading home. While MirrorPeak would be getting a new trainee doctor in the next few months, she would need a lot of supervision before he could think of taking any time off.

Not that he really needed time off. His work was his life, but maybe he could finally visit some of the other dragon clans nearby and see what their doctors were up to. His clan leader, Rio, had suggested it after meeting with David Lee and Wes Dalton of clans StoneRiver and PineRock, respectively.

However, none of that could happen until the new doctor arrived, and he most certainly shouldn't go check on Lexi and Ethan to see how they were doing. What if he had another life-saving surgery come up?

His dragon spoke up. *There could always be an*

emergency. *And our nurses know how to stabilize and triage better than probably any other clan, because we've been shorthanded for so long. We have time to check on the boy.*

His inner beast was the one person he could never lie to, so he mentally sighed. *I just want to make sure he's doing okay. He looked so happy earlier, and even if I can't take care of him, I want him to do well here.*

With help from Aunt Rita, we could raise him. And once you win over Lexi, we could be a family.

Not this again.

She should be ours, no matter if you deny it or not. I think she's our true mate.

A dragon-shifter's true mate was their best chance at happiness. Not guaranteed, of course. But the one downside was he would never know for certain if Lexi was their true mate until he kissed her. Because if Lexi was theirs, and he kissed her, it would start a mate-claim frenzy that wouldn't end until she was pregnant with his child.

And he'd only just learned he had a son, and could barely handle that news.

His dragon spoke again. *Regardless of what kissing her means, you like her.*

I don't know her.

Then fix that. Or are you really going to make excuses and lose our chance? The one you used to dream of, before the incident?

The incident was bloody worse than you make it out to be, dragon.

We were young, made a mistake, and the dragonman still lives. He's forgiven us, so why can't you forgive yourself?

Kyle didn't want to talk about it, and before he could think of an excuse, he heard a familiar female voice.

"Kyle! There you are. I thought I'd never find you."

He turned to see his Aunt Rita power walking toward him. She was in her fifties, with blonde hair that was lighter than when she was younger because of the grays, and eyes that were the same green as his own.

And despite the day's bombshell news, his aunt's smiling face made him smile back. "Hello, Aunt Rita."

He leaned down so she could kiss his cheek. Once he stood, she poked his chest. "I heard something from Rosa Maria, who heard it from her daughter-in-law. What's this about you having a son?"

"Keep it down. It's not supposed to be widely known."

She raised her eyebrows. "Then come inside and start talking."

Her small house was a two-minute walk away. Considering this wasn't his usual route home, maybe he'd unconsciously wanted to discuss Ethan with somebody.

Her house was green, complete with her prized rose-bushes out front. Once inside, the familiar clutter of family pictures, pastoral scene paintings, and bird statues instantly made him relax.

Once he'd sat at the kitchen table—his aunt always had her "discussions" at the table—she laid a plate of cookies between them and quirked an eyebrow.

With a sigh, he picked up a double-chocolate chip cookie and asked, "How much do you know?"

"Only that a DOCS employee showed up with a young boy who is your son. Did you know about him?"

"Of course not! I might not have wanted to be a father, but I never would've abandoned any kid of mine, if I'd known."

"But I heard you don't want to raise him. Is that true?"

He broke off a piece of cookie and tossed it in his mouth. After he swallowed, he replied, "I don't know."

"What don't you know, Kyle? You're a good male, under all that grumpiness. And who wouldn't be grumpy, given how hard you work? But if the boy is here with DOCS, then it means his mother gave him up."

"Yes. And by the sounds of it, the male who raised him didn't want anything to do with him, once he found out."

His aunt's voice softened. "So he was abandoned by two parents, then."

"Yes. And maybe if there was another doctor, I'd consider it. But there isn't. And too many people depend on me, Aunt Rita. I can't risk it."

"You won't repeat the mistake from your past, my

boy. This is different. You're not young and stupid, thinking you could live your old life and still be a doctor. You've grown up." She sipped the water in front of her before adding, "Plus, I heard the female DOCS employee is nice and pretty and good with kids. She obviously doesn't hate our kind, and she's single."

"How did you...Oh, wait. Jenny."

Jenny's mother-in-law was Rosa Maria Torres, his aunt's best friend.

His aunt continued. "Jenny won't tell anyone else, but she tells her mate and mother-in-law everything. Rosa Maria only talked with me because she knows how you try to carry the world on your shoulders and thought I might be able to help you. If you do want to raise him, Kyle, I would always be here to help you."

He sighed and ran a hand over his face. "I know that, but it's not as simple as raising the boy, though."

His aunt merely waited, nibbling on a cookie, as he debated telling her his dragon's guess.

His beast spoke up. *Why hold back? She'll find out eventually, anyway. She always does.*

Aunt Rita placed a hand over his and squeezed. "Tell me, Kyle. I can't help you if you don't talk to me."

He met the green eyes so like his own and said, "My dragon thinks the DOCS employee, Lexi Sakamoto, is our true mate."

Her pupils flashed to slits and back. "Hmm, then I think fate had a hand."

"Which is the problem. I like things planned,

without any surprises. I only just found out I have a son, and on the same day, I meet the female who's probably my true mate? After so many years of being in control, I don't like it."

His aunt snorted. "Come on, Kyle, you know how I found my mate all those years ago. It wasn't exactly convenient back then, either."

His uncle had been dared to visit a different clan, claim their clan's flag, and return to SkyFalls without being seen.

Except his aunt had caught him in the act and chased after him. He eventually tripped, she reclaimed the flag, and they'd ended up talking for hours. Somehow the incident had turned into secretly dating, which had been risky. Mating between clans back then had been difficult, and yet somehow his aunt had been able to stay on MirrorPeak and get her eventual mate to come, too.

He said, "But you were at least a little in love with him before he told you that you were his true mate. In my case, Lexi will be gone in two weeks, and I can't distract her from taking care of Ethan."

"Then why not get to know the boy, which will also mean spending time in her company, and see how it goes?"

"And what about the clinic?"

"Hmm. Rio owes me a favor, so I'll ask him to find another clan doctor to stay here and help for a week or two."

He raised his eyebrows. "Why does Rio owe you a favor?"

She waved a hand in dismissal. "That's not important. But I might be able to get someone here in the next day or two. If so, will you take the time to at least get to know the boy and think about telling him the truth?"

After taking another cookie, he nibbled and debated what to do.

His dragon spoke up. *At least give both of them a chance. Otherwise, you'll regret it. And if Aunt Rita does get another doctor here, you'll be out of excuses.*

You make it seem like taking care of my patients isn't important.

Of course it is. But every clan should have at least two doctors. Maybe one day they'll let humans train and live with dragon clans, and it won't be a problem any longer. But for now, Aunt Rita's offer is the best we could hope for.

Kyle met his aunt's gaze again. After a few beats, he sighed. "Fine. If you can get me some help, I'll spend some time with Ethan."

"And Lexi?"

He grunted. "We'll see."

"That's better than before." She stood. "Finish up the cookies while I call Rio. We'll have this sorted in no time."

As his aunt dialed their clan leader on her cell phone, Kyle wasn't sure if he was happy or anxious. He'd never thought to be a dad, and he was a long way from truly being one, and didn't know how to act.

His beast spoke up. *Ethan doesn't know how to be a dragon-shifter. So help him with that, and things will be fine.*

I hope so.

Soon his aunt hung up and told him that Rio would ask for another clan's help and sent Kyle on his way. Once he bid her farewell, he decided to head to the school and see if he could help the teachers. Or, at least, answer any questions if Ethan's tutoring session was over.

It was time to try and get to know his son.

Chapter Five

Lexi had liked the dragon teacher, Oscar Forrest, immediately. He was an older dragonman in his sixties, but didn't have a bias against all humans like some of the older dragon-shifters did, in Lexi's experience. Plus, he'd spent the last hour answering Ethan's questions as best as he could.

But as the boy's stomach rumbled, Lexi spoke in the next pause. "Ethan, we should go so we can get some dinner. Jenny said there's a restaurant here that serves pizza."

The dragon teacher nodded. "It's true. And it's wood-fired, so it's even better."

Ethan frowned. "What's wood-fired?"

Lexi answered, "That means it's made in a special type of oven, but don't worry, it tastes amazing, definitely better than frozen pizza."

The boy's stomach rumbled louder, and Lexi bit

back a smile before saying, "I'm hungry too, so say goodbye to Mr. Forrest, and we'll get some dinner."

Ethan said, "Thank you, Mr. Forrest, for helping me."

"No problem, Ethan. I'll see you again tomorrow, and don't forget to bring more questions to ask me, okay?"

The boy nodded, and after Lexi thanked the teacher, they headed out of the classroom and toward the exit. She asked, "What do you think of Mr. Forrest?"

"Well, he's nice, and he taught me a lot already."

Ethan hesitated, and Lexi said, "I think you'll have fun at school, but we won't rush it, I promise. And maybe you'll make friends at the playground after dinner."

"So we can still go?"

"Yes. It's nearly summer, so it stays light out for a long time. That was the rule I always had as a kid—we didn't have to go home until the streetlights turned on."

He bounced in place and cheered. "I like that rule! And I can't wait to see the playground."

She smiled and was about to ask what kind of pizza he liked when they exited the school and nearly collided with Kyle. Without thinking, she blurted, "What are you doing here?"

It sounded harsher than she'd intended, but he merely shrugged. "I wanted to check on Ethan and see if he had any more questions about being a dragon-shifter."

Ethan spoke up. "Oh, I have lots and lots. But first

we're getting pizza for dinner! A special fire kind, or something. But you should come with us."

Lexi was about to say he didn't have to when Kyle smiled. And for a second, she stopped breathing. The man was too handsome by half when he relaxed, even just a little.

Don't think about him like that, Lexi. Just don't.

Thankfully, he spoke and distracted her. "Only if Lexi doesn't mind. I know it's been a long day."

His gaze met hers, and his pupils flashed a few times. If she could only better read this man, but she supposed keeping his emotions tightly controlled was essential for a doctor. "You're welcome to come, if you like."

Ethan jumped up and down. "Yay, it'll be fun. Come on. Where are we going? I'm hungry."

The boy took Kyle's hand with his free one, and for a second, the dragonman froze. Maybe inviting him to dinner had been a bad idea, even if it had been Ethan who'd done it. And yet, the last thing she wanted was to force anything.

But then Kyle tightened his grip around Ethan's hand and nodded toward the left with his head. "The clan restaurant is this way."

They all started walking, and Lexi glanced at Kyle's profile and then at Ethan. Even if the boy's hair was a lighter shade, they had the same nose.

While they had a lot of physical similarities, their personalities were so different. And before she could think better of it, she blurted, "Were you just as serious as a child?"

Maybe she should regret it, especially as Kyle turned his head and arched an eyebrow. However, it was her job to better know Ethan's family. That's why she'd asked. It most definitely wasn't because she wanted to know more about Kyle himself.

He replied, "No."

But that was all he said, and an awkward silence filled the air. At least until Ethan asked, "Does it hurt to change into a dragon?"

Kyle shook his head. "Not really. It's a little strange at first, as your body and bones grow bigger. And it can hurt if you and your dragon don't work together. So you have to do your best to become friends with him now so you can be a good team later."

Ethan glanced at the ground and kicked a rock ahead of them as he said, "My dragon's kind of stubborn and loud and keeps trying to tell me what to do. I'm afraid to make him angry."

Kyle stopped and crouched down in front of Ethan. "The way he's acting right now is pretty normal, but you have to tell him when it's too much. If you don't, he'll get spoiled and it will be harder to become friends and work together. So maybe the next time he talks or shouts or throws a tantrum, ignore everyone else and talk to him."

"But won't people think I'm weird if someone talks to me and I stand there, not listening or answering?"

Kyle smiled, his pupils flashing, as he replied, "Here,

that's pretty normal. And you just saw my eyes flash, didn't you?" Ethan nodded, and Kyle continued, "Well, eventually you learn how to have short conversations with your dragon at the same time as talking with others. It'll seem hard now, but the more you do it and get to know your inner beast, the easier it gets. That's why you have to stand up to your dragon and treat him as an equal, and ask him to treat you the same."

"An equal?"

"Yes, as in you both get to talk, always discuss if he wants something you don't, and you try to make promises to each other to do things. Dragon-shifters call them vows, but it's like a really important promise."

"A special promise?"

"Yes. And once a dragon-shifter makes one, you always keep it. That's very important."

"There are a lot of new, important things, huh?"

Smiling, Kyle nodded. "Yes, but soon you'll be a pro, and maybe you can help the other dragon children understand humans better, too."

Lexi wondered if Kyle's words would trigger something about Ethan's past, but the boy merely bobbed his head. "I'll try. And the next time my dragon is loud or tries to tell me what to do, I'll talk back."

Kyle ruffled Ethan's hair, and Lexi softened toward the dragonman. For the first time, she was starting to see the doctor side of him that handled people who were injured or scared or unruly.

Under all that grumpiness and curtness was a kind,

patient man. Although why he tried to hide it sometimes, she didn't know.

Kyle looked up and noticed her staring at him—no doubt like some ninny—and she cleared her throat. "Shall we keep going? I'm starving."

Ethan said, "Me, too! I'm hungry."

Kyle nodded, stood, took Ethan's hand, and led them toward the restaurant.

And Lexi most definitely didn't look at Kyle's profile again, no matter how much she wanted to. One of the strictest rules of her job was that she couldn't dally with a dragon-shifter. She'd be fired immediately, and then she wouldn't be able to help any of the orphans.

Besides, it wasn't as if anything would happen with Kyle, anyway. She was just being silly and should maybe listen to her sister's advice about dating again.

So for the rest of the walk, she remembered all of her training and focused on the consequences of acting like an idiot around a handsome dragonman. By the time they reached the restaurant, she had everything under control.

Which was a good thing since as soon as she, Ethan, and Kyle entered the restaurant, all eyes went toward them and the room fell silent.

Kyle maybe should've realized arriving with Ethan at his

side, giving everyone a view of his mini-me, might've been a bad idea.

He hadn't intended to share Ethan was his son so soon. Eventually, everyone would figure it out as the boy looked too much like him to be anything else. However, he was still deciding what to do with the boy and only hoped everyone wouldn't mention to Ethan that he was with his birth father.

His dragon spoke up. *None of the gossips are here. And no one will want to hurt the child.*

Makayla, the youngest sibling of Chris North—one of the clan's Protectors—helped her parents run the restaurant. She walked up to him and said softly, "Thank you for saving Eli."

He'd barely saved Eli in surgery that morning. Regardless, Kyle never felt comfortable being thanked for doing his job. So he merely nodded. "You should thank your brother for getting Eli the help he needed so quickly. Your brother saved his life."

"Chris reacted about the same as you, meaning he brushed it off, but I'm still grateful for you both." Ethan squirmed a little, and Makayla glanced down, smiling as she asked, "And who's this?"

"I'm Ethan." He paused, glanced around, and said, "I'm a dragon-shifter, too."

Makayla's pupils flashed a few times, and she winked. "Well, that's a pretty awesome thing to be. Of course, I'm a little biased, since I am one, too." She looked at Lexi. "Although humans are okay, too. Well, most of them."

Ethan spoke up. "Lexi is nice and kind and patient. She helps kids like me."

The dragonwoman put out a hand to Lexi. "My name is Makayla North. I've heard about you but haven't had a chance to welcome you yet. It's nice to finally meet you."

Lexi smiled and shook her hand. "Nice to meet you, too." Ethan's stomach rumbled, and Lexi added, "We heard you have some delicious wood-fired pizza, and I think Ethan here is impatient to try it."

The other woman raised her brows. "Well, then, a growing dragon boy needs his food. Trust me, I know, I have three older brothers. Follow me. We have one of the best seats toward the back, where you can watch them make the pizzas."

"Really? I want to see! They said it was a fire pizza."

"Wood-fired, yes. A recipe from my grandmother, one people have tried to steal forever, but have never got."

As Makayla guided them toward the back of the room, Kyle nodded at various clan members. While some of them glanced between him and Ethan, no one blurted anything, thank goodness.

His dragon spoke up. *Rio probably told everyone to make Ethan feel at home and don't upset him.*

There's one clan member who wouldn't care. Thankfully, he's not here.

One of the oldest clan members didn't like change of any sort, and had been the loudest complainer about the other half-dragon child who had come to live on Mirror-Peak a few years ago. Since becoming clan leader, Rio had done his best to listen to the old male's concerns and smooth things over. But while Rio knew things were changing—especially given how much a book published originally in the UK about dragon-shifters had revealed to the human world—some of his kind would never change.

Before Kyle could worry too much about how the closed-minded male might treat Ethan, the boy finally spotted the big, open-aired oven in the back. "Look! They put the pizza in there with fire in the back!"

Kyle smiled. "I loved cooking over open fires in the summer, with my aunt, on the Fourth of July."

Ethan was too engrossed in watching the person making pizzas behind the glass to hear him, but Lexi said, "I've never really thought about dragon-shifters celebrating the Fourth of July."

He gestured toward the table, and Lexi sat, keeping an eye on Ethan. Kyle replied, "Some cities partner with local dragon clans and put on airshows, or so I hear. Maybe because Vegas and Reno are so close and full of drunk people who might forget the day and freak out, we don't do that here. But it's just a holiday to celebrate with the clan."

"I guess. My grandma never let us have fireworks,

but we'd watch the big displays sometimes. But flying dragons would've been better."

As she smiled at him, Kyle's heart thumped harder. Even though he barely knew her, he didn't hold back like he usually did and said, "I can give you a private show." He realized how that sounded and added, "For you and Ethan. In the air."

"Are you a secret daredevil, then?"

"I used to be."

As soon as he said it, he regretted it. Why was he sharing so much with this female?

His dragon spoke up. *You know why. The sooner you accept it, the better.*

Lexi looked about to ask him more details, so he said, "Ethan, come sit down at the table. Makayla's heading this way, and we need to order."

And so he managed to keep things light as they discussed pizza and listened to Ethan's enthusiastic words about the special oven.

If he was lucky, maybe Lexi would forget he'd mentioned anything about his past.

Lexi was fond of Ethan, but for a split-second, she wished he'd not heard Kyle calling him so she could ask what he meant about being a daredevil in the past. It was hard to imagine the mostly serious dragonman sneaking off to cause trouble with his friends.

But it was probably good Ethan had heard and sat down. After all, she needed to ensure Kyle would be a good parent, if he chose that route. However, she didn't need to know every little thing about him and his antics when he was younger.

Distance meant she could keep her job.

Dinner flew by, with mostly Ethan asking questions and Kyle answering. He was patient with the boy, always making sure he understood the answers. The dragonman also tried to bolster the boy's confidence when Ethan worried about him being raised a human up until a few weeks ago.

They had nearly finished dinner when a little boy of about six or seven walked up to the table. He had black hair and blue eyes, and looked a little like Makayla, but not quite. After raising his hand, the boy peeled back his fingers and revealed three little dragon figurines in various flight positions. He said, "My Aunt Makayla said you were new and had never lived with a dragon clan before. I thought these might help. We use them in class, sometimes. We can't fly yet, but they help us learn flight skill names and how not to crash."

As the boy moved his hand closer, Ethan gingerly picked one up. The small blue dragon had its wings out, as if it were gliding. Ethan traced the wings. "This is amazing."

"Yeah, I have lots of them, in all different colors and poses. We can share in school, if you want, until you get some of your own."

Ethan hesitated, and then smiled. "That would be fun. I'm behind, though. I was in a human school before."

"Then you can help me with human studies stuff. After school, you can come over, if you want to. My name's Jackson North. My dad is a Protector, and he knows a lot, so I know a lot."

"I'm Ethan."

Lexi noticed how he didn't share his full name, and she didn't blame him, considering his parents had given him away.

As the two boys continued to talk about the toy dragons, she glanced at Kyle and asked quietly, "Who's his father?"

"Chris North, one of the Protectors." He leaned closer, so no one could hear his next words, and it took everything Lexi had not to notice his heat or scent as he said, "His mate died in childbirth."

She wanted to ask how, but didn't want to risk Jackson hearing. However, a tall, somewhat fierce dragonman approached the table and grunted. "Jackson, you know better than to run off."

"Sorry, Dad. I just wanted to say hi to Ethan and help him. You always say to help people, and he needs a lot of help to learn everything."

Chris's face softened. "I know, son." He glanced up, nodded at Kyle, and then Lexi before looking back at his boy. "I have to drop you off at Grandma's so I can visit my friend in the clinic, remember?"

"Oh, I forgot. But Mr. Eli is okay, right?"

She studied Kyle, wondering if his expression would reveal Eli's prognosis. However, he merely said, "Eli is recovering from surgery."

Kyle shared a glance with Chris, as if neither of them liked what had happened. She burned to ask how the dragonman had been injured. Especially since if it was related to the League, her sister could probably help MirrorPeak, given her connections at ADDA.

However, Chris spoke to his son again before she could say a word. "Eli is stubborn, like me, and probably hates lying in bed all day. He'll be up before you know it, Jackson. But for right now, we need to go. Maybe Grandma will take you to the playground, but only if we hurry."

Ethan chimed in. "Lexi is taking me to the playground, too! Maybe we can play together?"

Jackson nodded and went to stand with his dad. "Sounds fun. And since Grandma likes to watch the skies change colors before it gets dark, we should have time to play a game. I'll see you soon!"

He waved goodbye, they all did the same, and the table fell silent for a beat before Ethan asked, "Do you want to come to the playground, Kyle?"

"I wish I could, but I need to check on some patients."

Ethan's face fell. "Oh, okay."

Her heart ached, but Lexi had dealt with more than one disappointed dragon orphan before, and quickly said, "You'll be so busy with Jackson that it'll be bedtime before you know it. We should go now, so you have time to play."

She stood, and Kyle avoided her eyes to focus on Ethan. "Have fun with Jackson, Ethan. I'll try to see you tomorrow, if I can. But you know I'm a doctor, right?" The boy nodded. "Well, sometimes things happen and I have to stay at the clinic for a really long time. But I promise to see you again soon."

"Promise?"

Kyle bobbed his head. "I vow it. I'll see you soon. Good night to you both."

He picked up the bill, headed to pay, and Lexi resisted frowning. Why was Kyle ignoring her?

She didn't have time to read his hot and cold moods, so she took Ethan's hand and guided him out, toward the playground they'd passed earlier. She needed to stop thinking and wondering about Kyle, and solely focus on her charge. If she did that, she might even learn some more about dragon-shifters.

Yes, learning more to help with other cases was more important. Even if she was curious about Kyle's supposed daredevil past.

Chapter Six

Three days later, Lexi wanted to storm into the clinic, find Kyle Baker, and scold him for avoiding Ethan.

The first day they'd arrived, he'd spent nearly the entire day with the boy, making a big impression. To the point Ethan kept asking after him. Every time Lexi had to gently say Kyle must be busy at the clinic, the boy had wilted a little.

Since she didn't have a phone number and she'd been busy with both Ethan and checking in with the clan leader and the Protectors, Lexi hadn't had a chance to try and see the dragon doctor in person.

What she couldn't understand was the radio silence. As a doctor, Kyle should understand how important stability was to a child who'd recently been abandoned. If the dragonman hadn't wanted to be a part of his son's life, he should've started as he meant to go on.

Because now, it would make everything that much harder if Kyle decided he was too busy to spend time with Ethan. She knew a little something about that.

After all, Lexi still remembered her first birthday after her mother had left her and Jennifer at their grandmother's house, when she'd gotten a birthday card. It'd given her hope that her mom would return. And yet, as each birthday passed without another word, it only reminded her of how much she was unwanted.

It was something she didn't want any of her charges to feel. Well, more than they already did, if they were given up at a later age.

The one good thing from the past few days was Ethan and Jackson had become fast friends, to the point she'd left Ethan with Jackson and his grandmother for a few hours. Lexi had liked the older dragonwoman the first day, with her no-nonsense attitude and secret stash of candies she gave out when she thought no one was looking.

With her free time, Lexi intended to finally hunt down Kyle and tell him he needed to make up his mind about Ethan. Maybe not about parenthood just yet, but if he was going to be a part of the boy's life, he needed to be consistent.

She reached the clinic, took a deep breath, and willed her temper to cool. Shouting didn't accomplish anything, especially with those who weren't at fault and merely worked at the clinic.

After asking to speak with Dr. Baker at the front

desk, she resisted pacing as the dragonman called someone. A few minutes later, a woman in her early 30s, with black hair and light brown skin, walked up to her. She had the white lab coat of a doctor, but before she could ask, the woman spoke up.

"Dr. Baker is getting some much needed rest. What can I help you with? Is the boy okay?"

"Er, who are you?"

The dragonwoman didn't so much as smile. "I'm Dr. Alvaro."

"Alvaro? Wait..."

"Yes, Rio and Solana are my cousins. I live with a different clan, but I'm here temporarily. Are you here about the boy?"

"No. I mean, yes." She glanced around. "Can we talk in private?"

"I have a few minutes, nothing more. Follow me."

Lexi followed the dragonwoman, more than curious about Kyle needing rest. Had there been an emergency? If so, she hadn't heard anything.

Once they entered a small office, Dr. Alvaro leaned against the desk and quirked a dark eyebrow in question. Lexi resisted clearing her throat and asked, "Did something happen?"

For a few beats, the dragonwoman said nothing as her pupils flashed to slits and back. Eventually she replied, "It's been hectic, is all you need to know."

"Wait, you do know who I am, who I brought, and why I need to talk with Kyle?"

"I may be a guest here, but yes, I know the boy is his biological son. Regardless, Dr. Baker finished a twelve-hour surgery only a few hours ago, the second surgery in as many days, and desperately needs to rest. He'll contact you when he can. That's all I can share."

Part of her admired the dragon doctor for protecting her patients and what happened inside the surgery. And yet, another part of her wanted to know if Kyle had saved his patient or not. If not, then she could only imagine how he felt, and he wouldn't be in the mood to try and charm a little boy.

Lexi's lingering anger and irritation faded away. Why hadn't anyone told her Kyle had been busy trying to save someone's life?

Then she realized the answer: she was a human, the outsider. It shouldn't sting, and yet it did, because it meant all the years she'd spent trying to help the dragon orphans didn't count for much.

Stop it, Lexi. Now's not the time. She focused on Dr. Alvaro and nodded. "I understand you can't tell me the specifics. However, can you tell me if Kyle went home or not? That way, I know where to check in with him later."

The dragonwoman tilted her head, her pupils flashing, and studied her. Why, Lexi didn't know, but she eventually nodded. "Yes, he's at home. Now, excuse me. I have a patient that needs me."

Dr. Alvaro gestured, and Lexi took her cue, exiting the room and heading back toward the entrance. Once she was outside, she hesitated. Would Kyle mind her checking in on him? If he didn't answer the door, she could just go back to Ethan and wait until he was rested.

She shouldn't care, she really shouldn't. And yet, she'd learned over the last few days that Kyle kept himself apart from most of the clan. Partly because he needed to, in order to treat them effectively. But partly for another reason, something no one would share.

As she dithered in front of the clinic, an older dragonwoman in her sixties stopped in front of her. Her eyes were the same green as Kyle's, although her hair was a light blonde to his light brown.

She spoke before Lexi could even say hello. "You're Lexi Sakamoto, aren't you?"

"Er, yes."

"I'm Rita Gibson, Kyle's aunt. He's not here, my dear. But I'm on my way to see him, if you want to come with?"

"Is he okay?" she blurted before she could think better of it.

Rita nodded. "For the most part, yes. Just tired and stressed." She lowered her voice. "He's had a difficult case lately, which is why I'm on my way to cheer him up a bit." She raised the tote bag in her hand. "I made all his favorite cookies and some brownies, too. He tries to hide it, but my nephew has a huge sweet tooth. I made way too many, though, so there's plenty for you too. Do say you'll come."

She should leave him alone. And yet, at the expression in the dragonwoman's eyes, she didn't think so she could say no. "If you think he won't mind."

"Not at all, I promise you." Rita looped her arm around Lexi's and tugged gently. As they walked, the dragonwoman added, "I know the truth about Ethan, and I think Kyle will want to raise him. He's just getting used to the idea."

Lexi blinked, glad no one was around to hear them. "I'm not here to force him to do anything, one way or the other. Besides, Rio said there are a few couples who might take Ethan in, and he's setting up some meet-ups for next week, if Kyle decides he can't do it."

Rita glanced at her. "What do you think of my nephew?"

It wasn't as if she could say one minute she wanted to scold him and in the next she wanted to lean closer as he whispered in her ear, surrounding her with his heat and scent, before pulling her into his lap and holding her close.

She still hadn't forgotten her dream last night, which ended up with Kyle's fingers doing amazing things between her thighs.

Stop it, Lexi. She'd barely known the guy a day, and it was getting ridiculous.

Rita snorted. "That complicated, is it?"

"No. Yes. No, I definitely mean no. It's just as a DOCS employee, I have to watch and document everything, so it's not as simple as someone being nice or not."

"I understand that better than you think, dear. I used

to work the front desk inside the Protector building, and I had to learn to judge someone's character and determine if they were a threat or not. Things are much better these days, albeit not perfect. Still, at least the clans talk to each other now. I had to move heaven and earth to mate my Johnny back in the day, since he was from Clan SkyFalls."

As Lexi listened to Rita tell the story about meeting her true mate, she couldn't help smiling. No doubt the young dragonman had been surprised, to say the least.

Once Rita finished, Lexi said, "That's quite the story, for sure. Almost like something out of a book."

Lexi also read between the lines—with a true mate, Rita should've had at least one child. But the dragonwoman hadn't mentioned any, only Kyle.

Just thinking about how this woman might've lost her baby made Lexi's heart squeeze.

However, they approached a dark blue house and Rita's voice garnered her attention again, "This is Kyle's place. He might be asleep, but you can wait on the porch while I check."

As Lexi sat on the porch swing, she rocked gently, admiring the view of the trees and the mostly clear skies above. A few dragons flew overhead, and she wondered what it might be like to fly somewhere with her own wings.

She'd spent so many years living close to Stockton in California and Reno in Nevada for her DOCS jobs that she'd forgotten what the mountains could be like—

peaceful with clean air, dragons overhead, and birds chirping.

Rita came back out and gestured. "He's awake, as I'd thought." She lowered her voice. "He rarely sleeps much after long surgeries. Probably because he has no one to talk to or share his troubles, so he overanalyzes everything in his head. Not that I should mention that. At any rate, come on."

Lexi resisted a frown and entered the house before following Rita down the hall. Since the house was older—probably about fifty years—it wasn't an open plan like most new houses, so the kitchen and dining nook were behind a door. Inside, Kyle sat at the kitchen table, a closed book in front of him, sipping from a mug when he spotted her. "What is she doing here?"

Rita opened her mouth to answer, but Lexi beat her to it. "And to think I was worried after visiting the clinic."

"I didn't ask you to worry."

"Not for you, but about Ethan," she lied. Well, mostly. She *had* gone because of Ethan.

Kyle sighed, rubbed a hand down his face, and replied, "I know. I didn't avoid him on purpose, I promise. It's been a difficult few days."

He sounded bone-weary, and it was on the tip of her tongue to ask more when Rita moved to the door and said, "I put the cookies and brownies on the counter, and now that Lexi is here to visit, I can meet up with Rosa

Maria like I promised. I'll drop by later, Kyle. Nice to meet you, Lexi."

With that, Rita left them alone. Lexi glanced at Kyle, only to find him watching her with flashing dragon eyes. His usual "doctor facade," as she called it, was gone, and he looked almost defeated. Even though she shouldn't, she asked, "What happened? And don't say nothing, because it's written all over your face that something did. Did your patient die?"

He studied her, but Lexi never looked away. For reasons she didn't understand, she wanted him to answer her. Maybe because it would help him be a little less alone with carrying the burdens of a clan doctor. Or maybe because if he was a little less weighed down with the world, he might take in Ethan.

Yes, that was the reason. The only one.

And so she sat and waited for him to answer.

Kyle eyed the pretty female sitting across from him, debating what to do. The last few days had been pure hell, with Eli coding and Kyle having to do multiple surgeries to keep the dragonman alive. And while he was fairly sure they were past the worst of it, Eli still had a long recovery ahead of him. One that Kyle didn't envy, not at all.

Dr. Carmen Alvaro had told him to take two days off, brooking no arguments. She was fierce, skilled, and even more closed-off than he was. However, she was also his clan leader's cousin, and if Rio said they could trust Carmen, Kyle would do it.

He'd planned to read to try and forget the last few days, but after reading the same paragraph twenty times, he'd given up. His mind kept straying to Ethan and Lexi, and especially how being with them both had felt so... right.

Which fucking terrified him.

So when she asked what happened, about whether his patient had died, his dragon spoke up. *Don't push her away. Just tell her the truth. And not just for me or even you, but for our son. We'll be no good to anyone until you relax and stop replaying what went right or wrong.*

Too tired to argue with his inner beast, Kyle sighed and answered Lexi's question. "You probably know by now that Eli was the injured Protector?" She nodded, and he continued, "Well, I've spent the last two days trying to keep him alive."

He paused, as images came back of beeping machines and him shouting orders. Lexi's hand covered his, bringing him back, and he met her gaze. At the concern there, he blurted, "I thought he was going to die, Lexi. He nearly died, and it brought back..."

"Brought back what?"

Was he really going to talk about *that*?

His dragon sighed. *Why not? She should be ours and know everything. Don't fuck this up.*

As Kyle searched Lexi's gaze, he saw the curiosity

burning there. And yet, she wasn't demanding or asking anything else, but waiting. Almost as if she expected him to brush it aside.

Which he didn't like. Not one bit.

So he finally answered, "I nearly lost a patient when I was younger."

"Nearly?"

He nodded. "He survived, but I almost killed him, all because I was young and stupid and too willing to prove myself to people who didn't really matter."

Lexi removed her hand, and he nearly reached for it, but held back. Of course she didn't want to touch him or offer sympathy. Given her job, she had no patience for reckless, selfish individuals. And he'd been both.

His dragon spoke up. *That was nearly a decade ago. Stop beating yourself up over it!*

Lexi's voice prevented him from replying to his beast. "Well, tell me what happened, and I'll be the judge."

His gaze met hers, and he didn't see disgust or judgment. No, only interest and skepticism.

His dragon spoke again. *Tell her. Then you'll see when she takes my side that it's more than time for you to let it go and start living again.*

Fine, I'll tell her. But she'll be on my side, you'll see.

Then get on with it.

"About ten years ago, friends dared me to drink five shots in a row before attempting one of my daredevil flight maneuvers. I didn't land as I should have, and I sprained several muscles. Right as I was hobbling back home, I got a call about a clan member's appendix bursting. I was the only clan doctor since the former one had just died, and I should've taken the responsibility more seriously. But since I hadn't, that meant sobering up as much as I could to try to save the dragonman. Because when an appendix bursts for dragon-shifters, it releases a nearly-fatal level of dragon-shifter hormones into the body. Calling another doctor would've taken too long, and so I performed the surgery, even with my hands shaking." He ran a hand through his long hair. "As it was, I had to open him up again the next day and repair something I'd damaged. It could've all been avoided if only I'd taken my job seriously. And on that day, I vowed to never do anything that could jeopardize my clan members again."

Silence fell, and for a few beats, Kyle avoided Lexi's gaze and stared into his tea. He fully expected her to stand, say he would never be a good father for Ethan, and leave.

Then her voice filled the air. "I heard you were only twenty-two when you became the clan's only doctor. Is that right?"

He met her eyes, frowning. "What the hell does that matter?"

"I heard you finished your doctor training quicker than most because you're really smart. And by any standard, twenty-two is young for shouldering such a great burden alone. No, you weren't a child. But dragon-shifters don't fully mature until age twenty, so still young. And I'm guessing you learned from your mistake, but instead of embracing that, you've been punishing yourself ever since?"

His dragon sighed. *See? I told you. She gets it.*

Kyle ignored his beast and narrowed his eyes at the female. "Not punishing, but being fucking responsible."

"By staying away, having no friends, and being lonely? And how does that help anyone? A sad, isolated doctor can only go on for so long."

"Stop trying to make excuses for me."

Her eyes flashed with anger. "I'm not making excuses! Trust me, I've seen my fair share of grown-ass people making shit up about why they can't take responsibility for a child. One that had no choice about being brought into the world, and yet they easily hand the child over to DOCS when they learn the boy or girl is a little different and has an inner dragon." She pointed a finger at him. "You, on the other hand, are punishing yourself for something you already took responsibility for and learned from. I'm not saying go out and get wasted every night, obviously. But it's okay to have a little fun, Kyle. To laugh and have a good time with others. That will do your clan more good in the long run."

He leaned over the table, bracing his hands on the surface, until his face was about six inches from Lexi's. Ignoring the scent of female and something floral, he focused on his anger. "Is this all part of your plan? To fix me so I can take Ethan, meaning you can leave sooner and get back to your kind?"

As soon as he said it, Kyle regretted his words, especially as hurt flashed in Lexi's eyes, quickly replaced with fury. She stood, the chair skidding behind her, and she growled, "Fuck you, Kyle Baker."

With that, she stormed out, and he sat down, holding his head in his hands.

His dragon snarled, *Why did you do that? She was genuinely trying to help, and you know it.*

I don't know.

Yes, you do. She was starting to get past your walls, trying to understand and help you, so you pushed her away. And not just any female, but our true mate. You really are *punishing us, especially me. I don't want her to go. You need to fix this.*

For a second, he nearly lied, saying he didn't want to change things. That Lexi had been wrong, and Kyle needed to constantly keep himself isolated so he could focus solely on being a doctor.

And yet, he'd met other dragon doctors, ones with mates and families, and they were no less skilled than him. Maybe, just maybe, he could ease his loneliness a little and still do a good job.

His dragon spoke again. *Make an effort. Life will be brighter with her and Ethan in it.*

Rubbing his face, Kyle sighed again. *I can't promise that, but I will apologize.*

Apologize and spend time with both of them.

And how can I do that? I've fucked up, big time. Lexi might not want to talk to me, beyond being professional and ensuring I won't hurt Ethan.

His dragon paused and then said, *Daniel was one of our best friends growing up. Talk to him. He might have some advice, especially since his mate has spent the most time with Lexi.*

Daniel Torres had been arguably the best of his friends as a kid. He'd even tried to stop Kyle from completing the ridiculous dare back in the day.

He replied to his beast, *I'm not sure he'll want to be friends with me again, after all this time.*

You'll never know until you try.

Fine. But I'm going to clean up first.

Good. And I'll think of how you can apologize and grovel, too.

And so Kyle took a shower and got dressed before heading out to visit his former friend, hoping it wasn't too late to rekindle their friendship. Because Kyle needed help, desperately, if he ever wanted a chance with his true mate.

Which he was starting to think he wanted, maybe more than anything except better knowing his son.

Chapter Seven

Lexi barged out of Kyle's place and took a long walk, needing to get her temper under control before she saw Ethan again.

By the end of the two hours, reason had returned to her brain, and she realized Kyle deliberately lashed out to keep people away. It still didn't excuse his behavior toward her or his accusation—he'd need to apologize and mean it—but after so many years, he'd probably forgotten what it was like to have or reach out to a friend.

And if there was ever a man who needed a friend, it was Kyle Baker. The only question was whether Lexi could be that friend or not.

Wait, did she want to put in the effort? But she quickly dismissed the doubt. Helping Kyle meant helping Ethan. Yes, that was it.

When she finally reached the main living area of the clan, where she was staying, she spotted Jenny Torres.

The woman waddled over, waving, and when close enough, she said, "Just who I was looking for!"

Doing her best to push aside the last few hours, she smiled. "Now I'm curious. What for? It's not Ethan, is it?"

"Oh, no. Well, yes, but not in a bad way, I promise. My niece, Reyna, invited Jackson and Ethan over for dinner. Daniel and his family are having a barbeque, and I thought it might be good for Ethan to meet all the kiddos and feel more settled. It was okay to invite him, I hope?"

"Of course. At this rate, Ethan will feel he belongs here within weeks, which is the goal."

"Don't go thinking you can leave just yet. That boy still needs you, after all."

Jenny couldn't know that Kyle had accused her of wanting to get away as soon as possible, and she knew the woman was only teasing. And yet, it still hurt a little to have everyone think she didn't truly care and only wanted to flee.

The other woman placed a hand on her arm. "Are you okay? I didn't say something wrong, did I? I do that sometimes, although I've been better at not being blunt with some of the older dragon-shifters. Still, things just come out, but I promise I never try to be mean or hurt anyone on purpose."

"No, don't mind me. It's just been a long day, and a barbeque get-together sounds wonderful for Ethan."

"Oh, did I forget to invite you? Because it's for you,

too. I need some more female support, for sure. Dragon-shifter populations skew male, and there are just too many of them, sometimes. Honestly, you think they'd remember to put down the toilet seat with a pregnant lady in the house! And yet, no. I nearly fell in a few days ago."

She smiled, doing her best not to laugh. However, Jenny sighed and added, "You can laugh. Daniel did, the jerk. Although he did make it up to me later."

As she sighed wistfully, jealousy shot through Lexi. But she pushed it aside. "I'll come, although just don't ask me to grill anything. I always overcook things, and the meat ends up like rubber when I'm done."

"Daniel takes grilling very seriously, so don't worry about that. You don't need to bring anything but your-self. We may as well head over."

"Now?"

"Yes, now! They're going to start a game of horse-shoes soon, boys against girls, and we need you."

She took Lexi's hand and tugged, and Lexi couldn't help but laugh. "You act as if the world will end if you don't win."

"It will, trust me. The Torres men are insufferable when they're smug. Well, dragonmen in general, if I'm honest."

As they walked, Lexi muttered, "And pig-headed, too."

Since Jenny was human, Lexi hadn't expected her to hear the words. However, the other human quirked her eyebrow. "Who acted that way, and what did they do? And don't look at me like that. I used to be a kindergarten teacher. Of course I hear everything."

Sighing, she glanced at Jenny, wondering how much to share. However, she was the only human on Mirror-Peak and was mated to a dragon-shifter. If anyone could give her answers, it was Jenny. And yet... "Promise me you won't tell anyone, not even your mate."

"As long as it won't endanger him or anyone here, I promise." She looped her arm through Lexi's and squeezed. "Tell me. Is it Kyle? And don't give me that look. I've seen how he looks at you, and vice versa, when neither of you thinks someone is watching. Are you his true mate and he's fighting it because he's a stubborn ass?"

She blinked. "True mate? Kyle's?"

"Well, he hasn't found her yet. Not that he's looked, or barely ever gotten laid, to be honest. He keeps to himself. Too much, according to Daniel, since they used to be friends."

Since Lexi worked with dragon-shifter children, she was well aware of what being a dragon's true mate meant —if they kissed, it would start off a mate-claim frenzy that would only end once she was pregnant.

And while she loved children, was she ready for her own? Especially if it meant giving up her job and helping countless children to find new homes?

Jenny's words interrupted her thoughts. "It's only a guess, Lexi. And as long as you don't kiss him on the mouth, nothing will happen. Still, I think you like him, and maybe you should use part of your time on Mirror-Peak to try and get to know him. Changing your life will be hard, I know, as I went through it all myself. But you don't have to make any decisions yet. Plus, didn't you say your sister worked with ADDA? I'm sure she knows what you can or can't do regarding your job, if you did mate a dragonman."

Her sister would probably know or try to find out. A flicker of hope, about still working with the children and maybe being a dragon's true mate, flared in her chest.

However, since Lexi didn't even know what she wanted—she barely knew the dragonman—she wasn't about to call her sister just yet. "For now, Ethan needs to be my focus. The rest I'll deal with as it comes."

"Of course. But if you ever need a friend and want to talk, I'm here. I know I can chatter a lot, but I can keep a secret when it matters, I promise."

As they approached a house with music and laughter drifting from the backyard, Lexi nodded. "Thank you."

"No problem. And now, I'll introduce you to my mate's family and then we can devise how to win at horseshoes. There has to be a way. I just know it."

They entered the backyard. And as Jenny's in-laws made her feel welcome, Lexi relaxed a little. The future could wait for an afternoon. She lived in the moment, laughing with Jenny and her mother-in-law, and smiling every time she spotted Ethan playing with his new friends.

Maybe, for once, things would work out without any problems.

Kyle had nearly reached Daniel's house when music and voices drifted from the backyard, along with the smell of charcoal and cooking meats.

He hesitated, and his dragon spoke up. *Don't run away. This is exactly what you need, what you've needed for a long time.*

What, to have everyone clam up and wonder what the hell the clan doctor is doing there?

No. Daniel and his family have known us our whole lives. I'll bet you the next destination of our weekly flight that they welcome us.

I could just let you fly anywhere.

Ah, but I want certain people to watch. Which means getting your act together first. Daniel can help, and you know it.

Fine. Whatever.

His dragon stood tall inside his mind, no doubt preening at being right.

Kyle approached the gate to the backyard, only for it to open, revealing Daniel's mother, Rosa Maria.

She was on the shorter side for a dragon-shifter, with black hair more gray than not, and dark brown eyes that could simultaneously peer into one's soul and offer empathy.

Smiling, she said, "Kyle! It's been too long, my boy. Daniel will be happy to see you."

He was about to say he doubted it, but held his tongue as Rosa Maria tugged him into the backyard and kept talking. "We're about to start a game of horseshoes. As I'm sure you remember, it can get pretty competitive. And even though you being here helps the male team, I'm glad you came. We've missed you around here."

He glanced at the dragonwoman, wondering how much his aunt had told her. Rosa Maria snorted. "This isn't some conspiracy. Yes, Rita told me a little, but you know I don't lie or offer pretty words, Kyle. And it's true —we've missed seeing you around. You always helped to bring Daniel a little out of his shell when you two were boys. Although I rather think it'll be the other way around now. Speak of the devil. Here he is to greet you. I'll leave you boys to it."

Rosa Maria gave her son a meaningful look and then hurried away. Daniel stood in front of Kyle and arched a dark eyebrow. "What happened?"

He frowned. "What do you mean 'What happened?'"

"You stopped coming to my family's get-togethers a decade ago, no matter how many times we invited you. So something must be up."

Guilt crashed down on Kyle. In his haste to become

a more responsible adult, he'd basically abandoned his friend.

His dragon spoke up. *Be honest with him.*

Kyle cleared his throat. "About that, I'm sorry, Daniel. It's just..."

After a few seconds, Daniel sighed and slapped his shoulder. "I know. Things went wrong, and you thought shutting everyone out would keep you on the straight and narrow. Am I right?"

"For a male who rarely talks much, you're chatty today."

"Am I wrong?"

"No."

"Well, there you go. So why today? And don't lie to me, Kyle. That's one thing I can't stand."

He was debating how to answer when laughter caught his attention, and Kyle glanced over Daniel's shoulder. There, with Jenny and the other females in a huddle, was Lexi.

Unlike with him, when she was sad or angry or pissed off—entirely his fault, of course—she was smiling and so full of light and life he ached to rush over and simply bask in her presence to ease his loneliness.

Daniel turned, followed his gaze, and then faced him again with a laugh. "What did you do?"

He grunted, and Daniel rolled his eyes. "You can be a grumpy bastard, but despite it all, you keep your huge heart well hidden, and I know you always want the best for people. Judging by your look, she's the reason you're here. So apologize to her, grovel, and then try to win her over. Is she your true mate?"

For a second, he thought about changing the topic. But after so many years of being alone, of keeping people at a distance, he didn't want to do that any longer. Even though his job meant being around others all the time, he had never really been a part of the clan. And he wanted that again, even just a little.

So he leaned close and whispered, "My dragon thinks so. But I fucked up, Daniel."

He squeezed Kyle's shoulder. "We all do sometimes. So apologize and sweep her off her feet."

"I want to, but then there's...my son."

Daniel's face softened. "I know it'll be a little more difficult than if it was just winning your true mate. However, if you want Ethan and Lexi, it's definitely possible. You'll just have to work harder. Are they worth it?"

"Of course," he blurted.

"Then you can start winning them over *after* the horseshoe tournament. It's males versus females, and we need you. Despite how uncoordinated Jenny can be at times, she's a natural at this game, and I don't want to lose."

At Daniel's sulky tone, Kyle smiled. "If a female who's seven months pregnant can beat you, I don't think there's any hope."

"Some friend you are."

"You wanted the truth."

Daniel snorted, and Kyle realized how much he'd missed his best friend.

His dragon said softly, *You have a second chance. Use it.*

Kyle put an arm around Daniel's shoulder and whispered, "Okay, maybe if we do this…"

And as they planned their strategy, Kyle's gaze kept drifting to Lexi, but she never noticed him. He only hoped she was a little less mad at him. But even if she was, he would start winning her over, no matter what it took.

Ethan spotted him, his eyes widened, and the boy ran over. When he stopped in front of him and Daniel, he said, "Kyle, you're here!"

He ruffled the boy's hair. "Sorry, Ethan. I've been busy helping people at the clinic. But I'm here now, and Daniel tells me we're on the same team. Have you ever played horseshoes before?"

Ethan shook his head. "No. I listened to the rules, but I still don't know if I can throw it right."

"Well, then let me give you some pointers. I used to be really good at this game when I was a kid, and I need some practice myself. Would you like to toss a few together, and I can help you?"

"Yes! I don't want to make our team lose."

Kyle took Ethan's hand and tugged the boy off to where all the males were together, and Daniel followed them.

For the next few minutes, he taught Ethan how to

toss the metal horseshoe better. With each cheer and smile from the boy, Kyle's earlier troubles faded a little. While he still needed to work for Lexi's forgiveness, the stress from his two days of surgeries melted away as he enjoyed being outside with his son.

As Lexi listened to Jenny and her sister-in-law argue about ways to distract the males to help their chances—there really were more of them—her gaze drifted, looking for Ethan.

She finally found him with the group of guys, which included Kyle. She nearly frowned. When had he shown up?

Kyle stood next to Ethan, gesturing with the horseshoe in his hand, no doubt teaching him how to throw it. When he grinned at his son, some of Lexi's anger evaporated. Oh, she was still mad at him for being so rude. But to see the dragon doctor outside, smiling and laughing with the other males, made her wonder if her words had made a difference.

Then Kyle's eyes met hers, and she could just make out his flashing pupils. Even though they were at least twenty feet apart, his intense gaze made her shiver. She wouldn't deny he was handsome.

And yet, attraction wasn't enough, not by a long shot. If he couldn't talk with her instead of shouting when he got uncomfortable, they had no future. Especially since being with him meant Lexi would have to uproot her life and maybe give up her career.

Eventually, she looked away and the game began, distracting her. Words of encouragement, cheers, and trash-talking made the time fly, and somehow, with Jenny's skill, they managed to take the game.

Jenny beamed as her mate rushed up to her. "I told you we'd win, even with fewer players on our team."

Daniel pulled her close. "How you do it, I'll never understand." His eyes widened. He moved back, and then he placed a hand over her protruding belly. "The little one is eager to come out and join in."

As Daniel led Jenny over to some chairs, Lexi couldn't hear any reply, but could see how much the pair cared for each other. She wondered if she'd ever find that.

However, Ethan dashed from behind her, snapping her out of her head as he said, "Next time we should hold a swimming contest instead."

"Oh, are you good at it?"

He stood a little taller. "I was the best in my class. The teacher said I had to be part fish. Well, before..."

His face fell, and Lexi's heart wrenched. Wanting to cheer him up, she gently raised his head with her fingers and said, "There are a lot of lakes nearby, smaller ones than Tahoe, and maybe in the summer you can swim again."

A familiar male voice came from behind her. "I'll

take you to some of them, Ethan, once it's warm enough."

"Really? When will it be warm enough? Soon?"

Kyle walked to stand next to the boy and ruffled his hair. "It should be in the next few weeks."

Ethan did a little dance. "I can't wait! I've never swum in a lake before. Do dragons swim in lake water?"

"Yes, and my beast rather likes it. He might even let you sit on my belly as we float on the water."

Lexi tried to imagine the scene, never really thinking about how dragon forms and children could interact and play. Oh, she'd slid down Kyle's side, but part of her yearned to also sit on his belly as they drifted over the lake.

Ethan and Kyle finished making plans, and Lexi debated if she should leave them. However, Kyle's green eyes met Lexi's for a beat, flashing between round and slitted, his expression serious. Before she could ask anything, he crouched down in front of his son. "Actually, Ethan, I want to make a lot of plans with you in the future."

"You do?"

"Yes." He cleared his throat. "In fact, I hope to know you a lot better and have a rather important question to ask you."

Lexi's heart skipped a beat. Had he really decided? Shouldn't he have talked with her first?

But as she watched Kyle smile at Ethan, she saw how much the dragonman already cared for the boy. Oh, she still had to stay around and make sure Ethan transitioned smoothly. But she sensed that if Kyle made a decision, he stuck to it.

Ethan, as if sensing something was going on, glanced at Lexi and then back at Kyle. "What? You're not going to ask me to leave, are you?"

"No!" Kyle said. "Of course not. I wanted to see if you wanted to stay with me, Ethan. I'd like to be your new dad, if you want. You can take your time to decide..."

Ethan launched himself at Kyle, and the dragonman engulfed him in a hug. Ethan's muffled voice said, "I want to stay with you. Please don't send me away. I like it here."

"Never, Ethan."

Kyle met Lexi's eyes, and at the fierceness mixed with tenderness, she knew he meant it.

Still, she needed to talk with Kyle privately about this, and soon. So she touched Ethan's shoulder, and he looked up at her. She smiled. "You'll be happy to live with Kyle, then? You can always take a little more time to make sure, if you need it."

"No, I don't need more time. H-he's like me. And he likes to teach me things, and we have fun together, and I don't think he'll hate me for my dragon eyes."

Lexi crouched down and placed her hands on Ethan's shoulders. "Never. I'm actually a little jealous of your flashing eyes. It means you'll always have a best friend."

His pupils flashed, and Ethan gave a shy smile. "I'm trying. He's still loud, though."

Kyle spoke up. "We'll work on that whenever you want, okay?"

"Okay."

Ethan noticed Jackson and Reyna waving at him. He looked torn between staying with them and going to his new friends. Lexi glanced at Kyle, and he nodded, so she said, "Why don't you get some dinner with your friends while I talk with Kyle?"

Ethan looked at Kyle. "You'll come over to the table soon, too?"

He ruffled the boy's hair. "I will."

Ethan nodded, hugged Kyle one last time, and dashed toward his friends. Once he was out of earshot, Lexi asked, "Are you sure? Because it won't just be fun times if you take him in. There will be tantrums and tempers and outright stubbornness. He's a sweet boy, but he's still just a kid, and they all have their moments."

"I know that. But I know what it's like to be a little apart from everyone, and I don't want that for him. I'm not sure when I'll tell him that he's my son by birth too, but for now, I want to give him a home." He smiled wryly. "He'll probably end up helping me more than the other way around."

They stared at one another for a few beats, and before she could stop herself, she blurted, "I'm glad you came today."

He raised his eyebrows. "You sure about that? Because I was a complete asshole to you earlier."

"You won't get any argument from me about that."

"I *am* sorry, Lexi." He sighed. "You were right, of course. And coming here today, being with Daniel, Ethan, and everyone, it felt...nice. More than nice. Almost like I'd been sleepwalking for years and am just starting to wake up again. Although there's one thing left I need to make up for, one thing I need to fix."

As he moved closer, her heart thudded louder. "Oh? And what's that?"

He traced her cheek, his finger leaving heat in its wake as he whispered, "I want a chance with you."

Ignoring the thrill that shot through her, she whispered, "Why? Because I'm your true mate?"

"That's not the only reason, although that's part of it. There's something about you, Lexi. Something that feeds my soul and makes me wish for more. I know there are a lot of reasons why it might not work, but won't you give me a chance? For at least as long as you're here? I'll do my best not to shut you out, I promise."

His pupils flashed rapidly, reminding her he was a dragon-shifter and if she said yes, her life would change drastically.

Part of her knew there must be a way she could still help the orphans if she stayed here, and part of her wanted to ensure it first.

The need for stability won out, and she finally replied, "Yes, but with a few rules."

His hand brushed against hers, and she nearly sucked in a breath. "Which are?"

"No kissing on the mouth."

He shook his head. "I wouldn't do that to you. If you stay, I want it to be because it's your choice and not because I've trapped you."

"I didn't think you would. And yet, given my job, I needed to hear it. There are dragonmen who have used that tactic, never telling the humans what would happen, and then later abandon the pregnant women. Many of them give up their children instead of moving to a dragon clan, and I have to deal with the devastated or confused children."

Anger flashed in his eyes. "If anyone from Mirror-Peak has done that, you'd better tell me."

"I don't think so, at least not from my cases—so many dragon-shifters visit the big cities for anonymity and come from a lot of clans. However, if I hear about someone from here, I'll let you know. ADDA might not be able to do anything, but maybe if a clan leader makes an example, it'll stop others from doing it, too."

He reached as if to take her hand, but withdrew. "Is there another dating rule that says we have to keep being together a secret?"

"Yes and no." His face fell, and she rushed to add, "I don't want to give Ethan any ideas, is all. I was that kid once, the one left behind and given false hope, and it's even worse when you're disappointed the next time."

He nodded and then grunted. "I understand, and I

wish I could take that pain away from you. But I don't like hiding something so important."

She smiled. "It's frustrating for me, too, if that's any consolation. Maybe it's being around dragon-shifters so much over the years, but I want to take your hand and make sure everyone else knows to stay away."

His finger discreetly stroked the back of her hand, and a bolt of electricity shot through her. If a brush against her skin did this, what would happen if they were finally naked?

Kyle's voice prevented her from daydreaming. "Meet with me tonight, then. Ethan already made plans to stay with Jackson and a few other boys. Come to my house, and I'll make you dinner."

"You can cook?"

"What do you think I've done with my free time? Read, of course, but I like cooking, too. It's relaxing."

She scrunched her nose up. "Glad you think so. I eat the same five things because it's easy."

"Well, tell me your favorite, and I'll try making it if you say yes."

His finger continued caressing the back of her hand, and she nearly leaned closer to his heat and scent. What was it about this dragonman that made her want to throw caution to the wind?

Not that she would. Still, she wondered just how much being someone's true mate affected things.

"So? Will you come?"

She nodded. "Okay. It's a date."

He smiled slowly until he grinned, and it made her belly flip. He really was too handsome.

"Good, and just in time since Ethan's waving at us to join him. But just know that later, I'm going to use all of my dragon charms on you, Lexi Sakamoto, and you won't stand a chance."

With that, he walked over to Ethan, and Lexi followed, somewhat stunned. Jenny pulled her aside and whispered, "Judging by your look, you two have made up. Now, come sit with me and I'll give you a few pointers on how to handle a dragonman."

And so Lexi went, although she kept stealing glances at Kyle as she ate. He gave most of his focus to Ethan, but every once in a while, he'd look up and smile at her.

Yep, she was in trouble. She only hoped it was the good kind.

Chapter Eight

While Kyle looked forward to better knowing his son and starting the adoption process, both man and beast were glad they could spend some time alone with Lexi. The fact she was giving him a chance, even after he'd been an ass, was something he wouldn't take for granted.

His dragon spoke up. *Good. Because she should be ours. Don't fuck it up again.*

I'll try not to. But it's not as if you've been helping, flashing images of her naked in our bed.

I consider it motivation. Maybe I should give you some right now.

Before he could protest, the doorbell rang, and he said quickly, *Behave. At least for a little while.*

We'll see. It depends on how you do.

Not wanting his dragon to give him dating advice,

Kyle went to the front door, opened it, and promptly forgot how to speak.

Lexi wore black jeans and a tight top that highlighted her slight curves. The top was dark blue with sequin things around the neckline, and it drew his gaze to her breasts.

Small, just a handful, and ones he wanted to worship with his mouth.

Lexi cleared her throat, and he met her gaze again. "Keep looking at me like that and I might do something I'll regret."

Once she was inside, he asked, "Which is?"

"Wouldn't you like to know."

She smiled, and he chuckled. "I would. But somehow, I think you're going to make me work for it."

"Damn straight." She sniffed the air. "Is that tonkatsu?"

He guided her down the hall. "Yes. I've never made the dish, and I have no hope of it being as good as your grandmother's, but I tried."

The deep-fried pork cutlet was simple enough, but getting the seasoning and the sauce right had taken some time. Especially since he'd had to ask around for all the ingredients in a single afternoon.

But as she entered the kitchen and rushed over to the plates he'd made—the pork cutlets were served with diced cabbage, a little dish of sauce, and rice—the excitement in her voice made it all worth it. "It looks so pretty!

And you even have sesame seeds to grind up, for the sauce."

"You said they made the difference. I had to try making the tonkatsu sauce, though, since it's not something they sell in the clan store."

"Where do you keep the spoons?"

He handed her one. She scooped up a little of the sauce and put it between her lips. She sighed in pleasure, and his dragon growled. *We could make her sigh even louder, if she'd sit on the counter and let us devour her pussy.*

Ignoring his beast, he moved behind Lexi and placed his hands on her hips. He stroked her side, and she leaned back against him. For a few seconds, he merely enjoyed the warm, soft female in his arms. "So? Is it good?"

"Almost as good as my Baa-chan's, but not quite."

"Baa-chan?"

"Oh, I forget sometimes that not everyone understands. My great-grandmother emigrated from Japan, and while my grandmother was born here, Japanese was her first language, not that anyone could tell since she didn't have an accent. And in Japanese, Obaa-chan means grandma, and Baa-chan is the more cutesy version, sort of like granny or nana." She turned her head and glanced up at him. "Make sure to tell me if I over-explain and you get bored. It's hard, sometimes, when something is second nature to me but others don't understand."

"I'm a dragon-shifter, Lexi. I understand more than you think."

Her smile shot straight to his cock. "That's true. Which means the both of us should just explain away, right?"

He tightened his grip on her hips. "Always. Don't hold back with me, Lexi. Ever. I need someone who isn't afraid to be honest with me, even knowing I might be a grumpy asshole about it."

"What, does no one hold the clan doctor to account?"

"You'd be surprised. Oh, my aunt and clan leader have no trouble telling me the truth. But even with dragon-shifters, some of them are afraid of doctors. And then there are those who think that if they get me mad, I won't help them, which is bullshit, of course. But when it comes to being sick or in pain, not everyone is rational."

She turned in his arms and placed her hands on his chest. He nuzzled her cheek, loving how she arched more against him. "So, will you be honest and possibly face the wrath of the clan doctor?"

"Wrath is a rather strong word." He ran a hand down to her ass and squeezed. She squeaked and then playfully hit his chest. "It's hard to think when you're touching me."

He quirked an eyebrow. "Do you want me to stop?"

"No."

He smiled and squeezed her again. "Good. Because

I've been thinking of holding you and teasing you since the barbeque."

"Hmm, me, too. And turnabout's fair play."

She ran a hand down his chest, down some more, but stopped at the waistband of his jeans. She traced just above them, each caress shooting to his cock and making him harder.

His dragon hummed. *Forget about dinner. Let's eat her instead.*

While Kyle was tempted to worship her with his mouth and have dessert first, this was more than a quick fuck. No, he wanted her to be his mate. And that meant more than sex, no matter how much man and beast wanted it.

So he kissed her cheek. "More of that later. First, the food's getting cold, and you're going to need your strength, given the way things are going."

"Someone's cocky."

"Have you ever been intimate with a dragonman?"

"Er, no."

He grinned. "Then you'll see."

She rolled her eyes, but allowed him to guide her to the table.

After he helped her into her seat, Kyle retrieved the plates and then the small bowls to grind the sesame seeds. He sat down and gestured. "Dig in."

"Or, as we used to say at my grandma's house, *itadakimasu!* It's a kind of thank you for the meal, although it literally means to humbly receive, but that's stuffy."

"Er, maybe you can teach me later. Right now, it sounds like I Eat Docky Moss, or something."

She laughed. "If she were still alive, Baa-chan would've laughed too." She dipped a piece into the sauce, took a bite, and moaned. "This is good, though. Especially since you've never made it before."

A thrill of pleasure shot through him at her praise. "I'm glad. Although I wish I could've met your grandmother, and not just because she sounds like a good cook."

Lexi's eyes filled with wistfulness. "She was an amazing woman. Barely five feet tall, but had a will of iron, for sure. However, I think she was always sad about not being able to help her daughter more. You see, my mom was an alcoholic. She managed to get her act together after meeting my father, but once my dad died in a car accident, she fell back into old habits and never regained control of her addiction again."

"It must've been hard to face that all as a child."

She picked at her food. "It was, but Jennifer and I were lucky since we had our grandmother, and I couldn't have asked for a better woman to raise us."

"It was like that with my Aunt Rita. She took me in, too, once my parents were killed by dragon hunters."

Hunters who'd wanted their blood and had left their dragon forms to the animals for days before his clan had found them.

His beast spoke up. *They found the people who did it, and they all died in prison. Don't waste time on ghosts when our true mate is right here in front of us.*

Glancing at Lexi, he took a deep breath and tried to tame his anger at their unnecessary deaths.

She placed a hand on his arm, and his anger melted away as she said, "I'm so sorry, Kyle. That's beyond awful."

He nodded. "ADDA spent a few years after that chasing away the dragon hunters from this area, but not so much in recent years. Probably because a lot of them are now working with the League."

She made a face. "I hate those bastards, and can't wait until all the hunters and League members lose their power and are prosecuted as they should be. The latter, especially, makes my job extremely difficult. But in some ways, the hunters are worse since they kill more often."

At the thought of Lexi being targeted by those assholes, he growled, "How have they made your job more difficult?"

She shrugged. "Since their goal is to drive all dragon-shifters out of the United States, they try to kidnap the orphans and drop them off in either Mexico or Canada—alone, in the middle of nowhere, with the full intention of them dying. I've only had a close call once, but it's happening more and more, to the point even ADDA is concerned. My sister tries to do what she can, but unlike her and Ashley Swift, not every ADDA employee is passionate about dragon-shifters. Too many just want a steady paycheck." She sighed. "I wish people would stop focusing on how we're different and look at how we're more alike."

Kyle reached across the table and took her free hand in his. He squeezed her fingers. "As a doctor, I know firsthand how people will always try to find someone or something to blame. Sometimes it's a coping mechanism, and sometimes it's just the inability for people to admit they were wrong or made a mistake. I try not to take it personally when they yell at me. But that's from my own kind, and I admit it's harder to see a human run away because they think I'm going to carry them off and drop them from the sky for fun."

"And yet you don't hate all humans. It's a big difference, I think."

"Well, I've met good and bad ones. Some may paint all dragon-shifters with a single brush, but I try not to do the same for humans."

"You're far more gracious than I am. I'm not sure I could see the potential good in anyone with the League."

"Well, I try to heal others, whereas you have to deal with abandoned children. I'd probably be more cynical, too, if that were the case. But you do so much good for the children, and to them you make a difference. Probably more than you realize, Lexi."

"I know, and most of the time, I'm happy with what I can do for them. I have far more patience for children, thankfully. Grown-ups, on the other hand, are harder for me to be understanding with. It's one of my many faults."

"And what are your others, I wonder?"

She arched an eyebrow. "Is this how you treat all your first dates? Ask them to spill the worst right upfront?"

"Considering I haven't had a date in years with a female I wanted for more than a night of fun, I guess so. I can list mine first, although I'm sure you know I'm stubborn, tend to keep things bottled up, and take any sort of mistake too seriously."

For a few beats, Lexi remained silent and studied him. Maybe he should've waited to be so honest.

His beast spoke up. *I think she'll appreciate it, given her job and all the excuses she has to deal with.*

Before Kyle could reply, Lexi shrugged and said, "Fine, I'll go along with your speed dating type thing. As for faults, I have a temper. It doesn't show all that often, but it does come out. I also..."

She hesitated and looked away.

Even though they were still getting to know each other, he didn't like her holding back with him.

His beast spoke up. *Coax her to talk. The more we know, the easier it should be to win and claim her.*

In agreement with his dragon, Kyle squeezed her hand and said softly, "Tell me, Lexi. Please."

Her eyes finally met his again, and he waited to see if she'd answer.

Lexi had never talked so easily with a man before, jumping from topic to topic, and revealing so much of herself so quickly. It was rather refreshing.

However, when Kyle had asked about her faults and she'd started to list them, she'd nearly blurted out her most embarrassing one. And the taunting remarks from her former boyfriends, about something being wrong with her or that she was too demanding, rushed forth.

Just as she tried to bottle those memories back up, Kyle squeezed her hand again. "Tell me, Lexi. Please."

Her gaze shot back to his, and at the kindness and patience there—mixed with his flashing pupils—gave her the courage to say, "I've never orgasmed with someone else, only by myself. And since I refuse to fake it, men take it badly."

She glanced away again, afraid to see his reaction. Would he curse her for being his true mate? Would he find a way to get rid of her? She didn't doubt that drag-onmen had egos just as fragile—or more so—than human men.

If he's scared away that easily, it's on him. Stop being a coward. That's not who you are. She finally met his gaze again, and Kyle's eyes flashed so rapidly she sucked in a breath.

Before she could wonder what that meant, he growled, "You've been with the wrong fucking men,

Lexi. And the fact they've hurt you with their words makes me want to find them and teach them a lesson."

His fierce tone tugged at her temper. "You say that, but I'm nearly thirty and no man has ever made me come. It's just something about me, and probably something you should know, if you want to try making this work."

With a grunt, Kyle stood and put out a hand toward her, palm up. She frowned. "What? We're not done with dinner."

"This is more important. Let me prove to you the other males were idiots and didn't know how to take care of their females."

Her heart thudded as she pressed her legs together. Surely he didn't mean...

Kyle added, "Yes, you're going to strip for me and let me worship that pretty pussy of yours until you scream in pleasure."

She'd heard of dragonmen being blunt about sex, but even so, his directness sent a shiver down her spine, in a good way.

And yet, she feared what would happen—or rather, wouldn't happen—and wondered if she could make herself that vulnerable or not.

His tone softened as he said, "I'm not like the others, I promise you. I'm determined, and patient, and a dragon-shifter. That'll make all the difference. Besides, I can tell you want it, Lexi. If you truly didn't, I wouldn't push. But let me be the first male to make you orgasm."

Even with his flashing dragon pupils, truth and determination blazed in his eyes. She'd never been with a dragon-shifter, and maybe they really were different.

As she stared at the tall, handsome dragonman, she decided fuck it, she wasn't about to pass up this chance. She might not have decided her future just yet, but for her, sex was an important part of a relationship, and it'd been one of the main reasons she'd ended things with boyfriends in the past. She'd just thought men, in general, didn't care about her if they got off.

However, as she placed her hand in Kyle's, approval and heat flared in his eyes. And for the first time in her life, Lexi felt as if she were the only woman in the world and that he might actually take care of her needs.

He helped her up. "The counter or the couch?"

She blinked. "What?"

"Do you want to spread your legs for me on the counter or on the couch?"

Considering Lexi's experiences had all been in a bed, her cheeks heated. And yet, the idea of her sitting on the counter and Kyle always remembering her as he cooked sent a thread of possessiveness through her.

Before she could change her mind, she whispered, "The counter."

He smiled slowly and tugged her to stand in front of a big, empty section. "Now, take off your pants. I'm tempted to slice them with my talons, but I don't want you walking around the clan naked later, showing every male your beautiful body."

For a second, she thought of asking him to turn around. However, she refused to be shy. If she was even considering a future with this dragonman—and she was—she meant to start as she would go on.

So she kicked off her shoes and slowly wiggled her jeans down, until she could take them off. She glanced at Kyle, and his pupils flashed even faster than before. His gaze met hers. "So beautiful. Hurry up so I can feel your skin against mine and taste your sweet honey for dessert."

She was torn between rolling her eyes and sucking in a breath. "You're direct."

His lips twitched. "I have to hold my tongue at the clinic a lot, but I won't ever do that with you again."

"Considering what you're about to do with it, I think not."

He chuckled, and the sound made her smile. She could get used to making the serious dragon doctor laugh.

Kyle reached out a hand and traced her cheek with the back of his fingers. "Take off your underwear and let me show you just what my tongue can do."

As the pounding between her thighs increased, she quickly stripped her panties and tossed them aside. Before she could ask what was next, he placed his hands at her waist and lifted her to the counter. The cool quartz surface made her shiver.

Leaning down, Kyle nuzzled her cheek. "Let me warm you up with my mouth, Lexi. Say yes."

"Yes."

He took her earlobe between his teeth and tugged gently, sending wetness between her thighs. Impatient now, she widened her legs and scooted to the edge of the counter.

Kyle chuckled, kissed her nose, and stood back. "I won't tease you this time, as I'm proving a point. But next time, well, I may keep you teetering for a long time before I let you fall."

Before she could ask what that meant, he ran his hands up and down her thighs, his skin warm and slightly rough, and she braced her hands behind her. He kneeled, and she noticed his hair was tied atop his head again. On impulse, she removed the tie, and his long hair danced around his shoulders. Not all men could pull off shoulder-length hair, but Kyle was so damn sexy, and she ran her fingers through it.

His hands never ceased stroking her skin as he murmured, "Getting ready to tug my hair and hold me close, love?"

She smiled. "Maybe. I was just thinking you look like a warrior of old with your hair down."

Taking her hand, he brought it to his mouth and kissed her palm. The fleeting touch made her stomach flip. "I'm yours to command, Lexi."

He looked at her expectantly, and she knew he wouldn't do anything unless she voiced her desires. Pushing aside her initial embarrassment, she whispered, "Then show me what it's supposed to be like."

It was vague, and a little bit cowardly, but Kyle didn't push. He placed his hand on her inner thighs, spread her wider, and leaned down to blow through her center. She sucked in a breath, the caress of air like a touch, making her skin even hotter.

Then his tongue was licking her pussy, each hot stroke making her moan. When he lightly thrust and retreated, she leaned even more heavily on her hands behind her.

True to his word, he didn't just lap at her, but devoured her. Each lick and thrust and groan he made only turned her on more. She never looked away from his determined gaze, his flashing dragon eyes making it more intense.

Never leaving her gaze, he licked up to her clit. The first flick made her jump, but he held her hips in place and strummed, until he found just the right rhythm, and she threaded the fingers of one hand through his hair and pulled him closer.

He chuckled, the vibration making her suck in a breath.

With a growl, he thrust a finger into her pussy as he continued to tease her clit, and Lexi felt the building pressure. Except unlike with her toys, this felt more intense.

Then he suckled her, and her orgasm hit, pleasure surging through her, wave after wave, so intense she cried out. Kyle never let up, drawing it out as long as he could, until she slumped, grateful for her hands on the counter to support her.

He finally released her clit and gave her entrance a leisurely lap. At his groan, Lexi opened her eyes. A mixture of pride and male smugness was written all over Kyle's face. "You're going to be cocky forever, aren't you?"

He stood, he wiped his mouth, and pulled her close. "Maybe, but I don't think you'll mind. I'll only be this smug again when you come and cry my name. That'll be my next challenge." After nuzzling her cheek, he added, "You fell apart easily enough for me, love, proving that the other males were fools."

She smiled, hooking her hands behind his neck and whispering, "I don't mind admitting I'm wrong this time. I'm glad, actually." She laid her head against his chest, his heart thudding under her ear, proving he wasn't as calm as he outwardly appeared.

"You'll learn soon enough that when it comes to a dragon-shifter and their mate, they will do anything it takes to make them happy, Lexi. And orgasming is just the beginning."

She wanted to argue, and yet, she'd seen Ashley Swift and her dragon mate together before, when visiting Clan PineRock for her job. Wes had always had Ashley's back, and yet did little things like remind her to eat or that she wanted to take their son to the playground. Not to mention he'd always gazed at his mate as if she were the most precious thing in the world.

She hadn't remembered about that for a long time. Probably because she'd been jealous and knew it'd been stupid.

But now, snuggling against Kyle's chest as his hands stroked her back, a sense of rightness fell over Lexi. Not just because he had a talented mouth, but simply cuddling in the kitchen, with the dinner he'd made specifically to please her still on the table, she wondered what she'd been doing up until this point. Apart from her family, no one had tried to make her happy, to put her needs first.

Yet despite their short acquaintance, Kyle had done more for her than any boyfriend in the past.

She should raise her head, thank him, and finish the dinner he'd made.

And yet, the more he stroked her back, the heavier her eyes grew, until she fell asleep in his arms.

Chapter Nine

The next morning, Kyle stood in the doorway of his guest room, watching Lexi as she slept. He'd fully expected her to wake up as he'd carried her from the kitchen the night before. However, even in sleep, she'd merely snuggled more against him and sighed.

At the sight of her slightly disheveled, trusting him enough to watch over her, something had shifted inside him.

He wanted her as his mate.

Not getting into bed with his human had been the hardest thing he'd done in a while. However, it would've been too easy to accidentally kiss her, or vice versa, and he hadn't wanted to risk it.

His dragon spoke up. *Soon she'll be ours completely.*

It was one night. Give it time, dragon. We have Ethan to think of as well.

Of course I care about our son. However, we have to woo Lexi, too. She is our female. Convince her to stay with us and be our mate.

Before he could think of how to do so in a way where she could keep her job—which was extremely important to Lexi—she moaned and rolled onto her back, stretching her arms above her head. What he wouldn't give to go over, pin her hands to the mattress, take her mouth, and claim her completely.

She opened her eyes, frowned, and then met his gaze. She squeaked and sat up. "Is-is this your place?"

He smiled, came in, and offered her the coffee in his hands. She took it, sipped, and he answered, "Yes. You fell asleep after your orgasm, and I carried you to my spare room. You never woke up, so you must've been tired and really relaxed."

She narrowed her eyes. "You still look entirely too smug about last night."

He laughed. "Of course I do. I proved you wrong in the best way, love. I mean, you did sleep through the night."

"Which is definitely weird, as I usually have trouble sleeping in unfamiliar places."

His dragon spoke up. *She had no trouble here because she knows she belongs with us.*

Ignoring his beast, he replied, "As much as I wish I could join you and make you come again, I have to go to the clinic soon and then check on Ethan. I have just enough time to make you breakfast, if you're hungry."

Her stomach growled, and he grinned. Lexi sighed. "I didn't finish dinner, and I'm starving. Please tell me you have eggs, toast, and cheese. It's my favorite bigger breakfast."

"What, do you eat lettuce some days or something?"

She rolled her eyes. "No, but when I have to deal with a new baby drop-off, I barely have time to grab a granola bar."

He moved and sat on the bed next to her, cupping her cheek and stroking her soft skin with his thumb. "Does it happen often?"

"Not as much these days. However, after a Tahoe Dragon Lottery, any of the women who don't get picked usually go looking for a dragonman in the worst places. Nine months later, there's a rush."

Every year, a dragon clan would offer a male and a female volunteer who would pick a human from a room and sleep with them, with the hopes of having a child. Whenever it was a dragonman's turn, the turnout was more determined than the other way around, and he'd heard stories of the dragon-shifter haunts in the cities being flooded with disappointed lottery candidates.

"I never really thought about that. You'd think the dragon males would be more careful."

Lexi shrugged. "You'd think. But I'm sure there are plenty of dragonmen, like human men, who refuse to use condoms because 'it doesn't feel right' or some BS."

"If they're going to be idiots, then they should step up when there's a child."

"I know. Most of the trouble has been with the clans in Northern California and Arizona. Both have refused to allow humans into their clans, no matter what. Anyone who dallies is shunned and kicked out. And while I haven't heard it myself, my sister tells me some of the dragon leaders are determined to form their own country somewhere inside the USA."

"Which is impossible and will make them a target of not only ADDA, but the US military as well."

She nodded. "I sometimes wish ADDA would host events where humans and dragon-shifters could mix freely and learn more about each other. In the UK they've held some successful children's events, but trying to do that here has been like trying to walk through a brick wall."

He raised his other hand, holding her face, and replied, "Somehow, we'll try to make that a reality."

"We?"

"I hope so. I know it's still early days, but I am determined to win you over, Lexi Sakamoto, no matter what. And given how your work is important and means so much to you, I need to figure out how to keep it a part of your life, too. Well, provided you consent to stay and be my mate."

As soon as he said it, Kyle wondered if she would freak out. It was rather soon, and yet the more time he spent with her, the more he knew he wanted to claim his true mate and make her and Ethan happy.

"It is early, but I very much want this to work, Kyle.

The main thing holding me back would be abandoning the orphans. So, yes, let's try to find a way for me to keep working with them if I do end up staying."

While he knew there was no "if" about it since he was determined to win his true mate, he merely smiled, kissed her cheek, and asked, "With that decided, how about breakfast? You're not leaving until you eat."

She quirked an eyebrow. "You're going to keep me prisoner?"

"No, I'll just call Aunt Rita and she'll fuss and make a big to-do, and you'll be waddling out of here by the end of it."

"Some of us don't have dragon-shifter metabolisms."

He stood, put out a hand. "Maybe not, but you can certainly eat more than a granola bar. Come on. I'll cook whatever you want, even if it's only eggs and toast."

She placed her hand in his. "And cheese."

"Yes, cheese." He tugged, and she stumbled against him. Kyle quickly wrapped his arms around her, loving the feel of her warm, soft body against his. As he nuzzled her cheek, he said, "Although I'm starting to think dessert for breakfast might be better."

Her stomach growled, and he leaned back. At the sheepish look on her face, he smiled. "You come first, though. Let me feed you before you faint and then I have to carry you to the clinic."

She rolled her eyes. "I don't faint. I might be human, but I'm not a porcelain doll, by any means."

"Of course not. You might have a huge heart, but

you're strong, in so many ways. Especially dealing with so many children wondering about why they've been abandoned."

Her face softened. "It's the hardest part of my job. But even if it's difficult, finding a good fit is what makes it all worth it. Like with Ethan. But I think as a doctor, you understand a little something about finding the good among the bad."

Tracing the curve of her cheek, he replied, "Most of the time, yes."

And with you as our mate, there would be a lot more good to look forward to, he left unsaid. He wasn't about to scare Lexi away.

His dragon huffed. *Just tell her.*

Not yet. Let's find a solution to her job issues first.

Jobs are one of those human things I'll never understand.

Ignoring his beast, he kissed Lexi's cheek, lingering for a second, before stepping back and taking her hand. "Come on. I have to leave in an hour, and I want to make sure you eat properly."

After he guided his female to the kitchen, she sat down and chatted as he made her breakfast. And as they sat together, he easily envisioned Ethan joining them.

More than ever, Kyle looked forward to the day he could finally make his own family and stop living so alone and isolated.

Chapter Ten

The next week flew by for Lexi as she balanced spending time with Kyle and ensuring Ethan was settling into life on Clan MirrorPeak. As soon as the paperwork was finalized, Ethan could finally live with Kyle full-time. And she couldn't wait.

She'd also become better friends with Jenny Torres. The woman had answered any question she threw at her about living with the dragon-shifters, such as if it was difficult being the only human, and she'd assured her most of the clan welcomed her. She'd also explained how it really wasn't that difficult, once she'd learned all the dragon customs, because her sister and brother-in-law visited as much as they could, giving her much-needed "human" time. ADDA was being more lenient about letting humans have their family visit them on the dragon clans, at least in the Tahoe area.

Jenny had also supported Lexi's dream of having

human and dragon children interacting at some sort of event, like in the UK with Clan Stonefire, and was coming up with some ideas, too.

In general, Lexi had been the busiest she'd ever been, and yet the most happy. Almost as if she'd found where she belonged.

Where she hoped she could belong.

Today, however, she needed to focus solely on her job and finish filing her final report on Ethan and Kyle's adoption. The meeting she had with some ADDA and human social workers later made her nervous, like it always did. They rarely denied the adoptions she supported, and yet, this wasn't just any adoption—Ethan was her potential stepson.

You'll do fine. Stop worrying about it and just be your badass usual self.

After a few calming breaths, she approached the school to pick up Ethan. She'd barely entered the front yard when children started rushing out of the building. All ages shared the same school, but the older kids had already gone home and just the elementary kids passed by her. A few waved at her—like Jackson, as well as Jenny's niece and nephew—but Ethan was nowhere to be found.

Once the last of the kids walked past her, she entered the building and found Ethan's classroom. Inside, Mr. Forrest sat at his desk, shuffling papers. When he glanced up, his pupils flashed as he smiled.

"Ah, Lexi! Have you come for another report? Ethan's been doing wonderfully well, thankfully."

"I'm glad to hear that, but I actually came to pick up Ethan. Is he meeting with some of the other teachers for extra lessons?"

Mr. Forrest frowned. "No. The boy was called to the front office earlier. I thought you'd come to pick him up?"

Warning bells rang inside her head. "No. And you don't know who it was?"

"Just that it was official ADDA and DOCS business. Ethan mentioned a meeting later today, and I thought they'd just come early."

Her stomach churned. This was bad. "No. It's not until later."

Mr. Forrest stood and rushed to the door. "Come on. I'm sure it's nothing, and maybe it was Kyle who came by. Let's find out."

As they strode down the hall toward the front office, Lexi's heart pounded. Her gut said something was wrong.

And yet, she would gladly be wrong if it meant Ethan was safe.

They approached the dragonwoman at the front desk, and she looked at Lexi and then at Mr. Forrest. "Is something wrong, Oscar?"

The teacher replied, "I don't know. Earlier, Ethan was called to the front office to be picked up. Who was it?"

The dragonwoman shook her head. "Ethan was never called to the front office, or showed up here."

Lexi's stomach dropped. "Are there security cameras inside the school? Ones we can check and maybe see where Ethan went?"

"Yes. Follow me."

Mr. Forrest gave Lexi a sympathetic look. "Maybe he ran off with Jackson, or one of the other boys. They all try to sneak away sometimes."

"But he's only six."

The dragonwoman led them inside a small room, equipped with various monitors. As she fiddled with one, she explained, "We have someone monitoring these in the mornings, lunch, and evenings, but we always record."

Even if she wanted to shout they should have round-the-clock security, Lexi knew sometimes there weren't enough people to fill all the jobs inside a dragon clan. It was one of the many reasons her sister kept pushing to allow humans to work inside them during the day.

Something she'd bring up to her big sister later.

The dragonwoman's voice garnered Lexi's attention. "There's Ethan, but I don't know who that is. Do either of you?"

Lexi leaned closer and scrutinized the man. Given the lack of a tattoo on his upper arm, he was probably human. "No, but he seems familiar somehow."

As she studied the man a little closer, it finally hit

her how much the man resembled Ethan, and she gasped. "It can't be. He lives in Idaho."

Mr. Forrest asked, "Do you know who that is?"

"I can't be 100 percent positive given the video quality, but I think that might be Ethan's maternal uncle—Patrick White."

The one who'd tried to take Ethan the day he'd been dropped off, but who had failed the background check and been denied. The man had been in and out of jail for the past decade, and his online accounts were full of dragon-related hatred. Plus, during his interview, his dragon hatred had shone through clearly, even for his nephew.

So why had he come here? Not out of some sense of duty of familial love, that was for sure.

Lexi took out her phone and said to the dragon pair, "I might know where he went. I need to go after him."

Mr. Forrest shook his head. "Tell the Protectors, Lexi, and they'll help you."

"I'll call them when I'm on the road, but I can't waste any time. Ethan is probably in danger."

Before they could persuade her out of her plan, she hit Call on her phone and power-walked toward where her car was parked. She asked a few things from her colleagues and learned that Patrick White was still staying just outside Reno with a friend.

After clicking End, Lexi slid inside her car, started it, and headed out. By now, the guards knew her and let her out without a word.

As she drove down the mountain, well over the speed limit, she willed for Ethan to be okay. Given how much his maternal uncle hated dragon-shifters, he'd probably use the boy for his own gain. Namely, selling him to the League, or maybe to the despicable humans who thought to collect dragon-shifters like pets and keep them in chains.

And she couldn't let either situation happen, no matter what.

Chapter Eleven

Kyle exited the operating room, cleaned up, and headed toward his office.

However, as soon as he set foot in the hallway, Daniel startled him as he said, "Kyle, why the hell haven't you answered your phone? I've been trying for over an hour. But whatever the reason, you need to come with me. Now. And don't ask questions until we're outside."

Given Daniel's serious tone, brooking no argument, Kyle kept his mouth shut and followed his friend. Once they were far enough away from the clinic, Daniel spoke again. "Someone took Ethan, and for reasons I'll never understand, Lexi went after him on her own."

His stomach dropped. "What? Tell me what the fuck happened."

Daniel filled him in on how Ethan's uncle had posed as an ADDA employee, took Ethan away, and then Lexi had gone after them. However, after a brief phone call, they hadn't heard from Lexi again.

His dragon growled. *We need to go after them.*

We're not Protectors, dragon, and can't do this alone. However, we'll go with them, in case Ethan or Lexi are hurt.

Kyle spoke aloud. "Is ADDA doing anything? Or DOCS?"

"We're working on that."

He stopped, pushed his friend against the nearest wall, and growled. "That is my mate and son you're talking about. Do more than work on it."

Daniel's pupils flashed before he replied, "I get you're upset. I can only imagine how I'd act if something happened to Jenny. But Rio and Axel are already working on a plan, determined to bring them both home as soon as possible."

Home. Yes, this was where they both belonged. And Axel was the head Protector of Clan MirrorPeak, and very good at his job.

His dragon spoke up. *Axel and Rio will do everything they can to bring them back, along with Daniel. Let him go.*

Kyle released his friend. "Sorry. But how close are you guys to a plan?"

"Close. In fact, we have help coming and need to get going to meet with them."

"Help? Who?"

"I'm not sure. But if Rio trusts someone to come, then that's enough for me."

Kyle nodded. "I just hope you know that I'm going with you. Yes, I'll stay in the back, out of danger. But I need to be there in case either of them is hurt and needs medical attention."

"As if we'd try to stop you. Just listen to our orders, okay? If it's related to the League or any of the humans who hate us, you need to be careful. Some of them don't care about killing, even if it means ending their own lives."

He grunted. "After Eli, I'll never dismiss humans again."

Not wanting to think about how they'd nearly lost their friend, Kyle followed Daniel to the Protector building. Once inside, they went to one of the conference rooms, only to find Ashley Swift and her mate, the Pine-Rock clan leader Wes Dalton, at the table, their heads together and talking. They noticed them and stood, their expressions a mixture of anger and concern.

Kyle blurted, "Have you found my son? Or Lexi? What the hell is ADDA doing to help them?"

Ashley still worked for ADDA, despite living with a dragon clan.

The female merely arched an eyebrow as her mate growled. She placed a hand on Wes's arm and spoke first. "Luckily for you, I know how testy dragonmen get when their mates and families are threatened, so I won't take offense. And we're doing plenty. Lexi's sister,

Jennifer, is doing everything she can to find out where Ethan is. Lexi's phone died at the last known address of Patrick White." Ashley quickly filled them in on Ethan's maternal uncle and continued, "Your clan has permission to retrieve the boy, as long as you don't kill anyone. Well, unless it comes to self-defense or death yourselves. But it'll be looked at closely, so I wouldn't recommend it."

His dragon spoke up. *Too bad.*

Ignoring his beast, Kyle replied, "Then why are we here, talking, instead of heading for this uncle's place?"

Ashley replied, "Because Ethan isn't there. Police discovered his uncle's place empty, except for Lexi's phone. Her car was still parked there, too."

His stomach dropped. "Please tell me you know where they are."

Wes finally spoke up. "We think the bastard uncle took them to a League outpost northeast of Reno, not far from the mining ghost town of Vernon. Our patrols found it by accident, when looking for a lost clan member a few months ago."

Ashley chimed in again. "I've tapped my trustworthy contacts inside ADDA and the human police, and according to them, they think it's some sort of dragon-shifter trading and deportation outpost. Rich humans come to buy the ones they want, and the rest get drugged and dropped outside of the country."

He clenched his fingers into a fist. "Then why haven't your people shut it down?"

"Because a human named Duncan Parrish owns the property and denies any illegal activity. And since he has a lot of money, he's buying off people left and right."

The door opened, and Axel and Rio walked in. Both nodded greetings at Ashley and Wes before Rio said, "Thanks to David Lee on StoneRiver, we know Duncan Parrish is out of the country on a business trip. Since we have permission to retrieve our clan members, we're going to leave as soon as everyone is ready."

Normally, Kyle would linger on Rio referring to Lexi and Ethan as clan members. It was what he wanted, after all. However, finding his female and son was more important. Kyle said, "I can put together a medical team and be ready in fifteen minutes."

Ashley spoke up. "You all need to be careful. Not that I don't think you're capable—you are. But Parrish is sort of my nemesis, and extremely powerful. Once you do this, he'll go after you, too."

"I don't care," he blurted.

Then Kyle realized this wasn't just him facing a new danger. He glanced at Rio, Axel, and Daniel in turn. Rio nodded. "We feel the same way. I've known about Parrish for a while now, and I don't like how much power he's collecting with money and favors. At some point, he'll piss off enough people and dragon-shifters that his influence will crumble. If we can help that along, I'm all for it."

Axel added, "Even if it means hell later on, I can't ignore the innocents about to be fucking sold off. We'll rescue your female and son, and the others, too. Parrish can go to hell."

Daniel shrugged. "Jenny would never forgive me for abandoning any child, let alone one she adores already. She knew when she mated me that it could be dangerous. Besides, we all help each other here, Kyle. And whether you've realized that we've had your back this whole time or not, you do."

His dragon said softly, *I told you we should've interacted with the clan sooner. They are our friends.*

Kyle replied to the males. "Thank you."

Rio lightly slapped his arm. "No thanks needed. Now, go gather your team while I talk with Ashley and Wes. We'll all meet in the main landing area in twenty minutes."

And so Kyle left, doing his best to focus on assembling his medical team and bringing the right supplies. Dr. Carmen Alvaro also said she'd prep everything, just in case they needed to operate.

Maybe before Lexi and Ethan, he might've balked at asking for help. However, knowing there might be someone else who could save his future family lifted some of the weight off his shoulders. Not much, given he was worried to death about what could still happen. However, Lexi and his dragon had been right all along— he needed to stop isolating himself so much from the clan.

His dragon spoke up. *She is ours. And not just because she was on my side.*

I agree, dragon. She is our future. Her and Ethan.

And Kyle couldn't wait to claim her officially. The female was not only good for him, he loved her. The time might've been short, but just thinking of life without her was unbearable.

And so Kyle headed toward the main landing area, more determined than ever to bring back his female and his son so he could start the future he'd never known he wanted.

Chapter Twelve

L exi woke up with a groan. Her head pounded, her wrists hurt, and it was extremely hot.

She struggled to remember what had happened. Because after knocking on the door of where Patrick was staying, there was a black hole of nothingness.

Ethan. She had been looking for Ethan.

Blinking her eyes open, she scanned the room. But her stomach dropped when she noticed she was alone.

Get a grip, Lexi. You can't escape and look for the boy if you freak out. Ethan needs you. So calm the hell down.

After a few deep breaths to tamp down her encroaching panic, Lexi was able to focus on her surroundings.

Light filtered through boards nailed over the window. The walls were bare and dirty, and the floor was covered in warped wooden planks that had definitely seen better days.

A low, unintelligible rumble filtered through either the walls or the window, which piqued her interest. However, Lexi struggled to stand with her head pounding and her limbs not wanting to work properly.

Once she was finally upright, she leaned against the wall to keep from falling and took deep breaths until her dizziness faded. Even though the room was extremely warm, the fuzziness in her head was no doubt from some kind of drug.

Just imagining that Ethan might've also been drugged gave her the strength to wobble across the room, to the window, using the wall for support. She finally reached it, and Lexi peered through the boards, but the windowpane was extremely dirty. She did her best to wipe away the dirt with her fingers and managed to clean just enough to see cars parking and people exiting them before heading toward some point in the distance.

One thing stood out to her immediately—every car was the same white make and model. Almost as if it'd been a requirement to come to wherever the hell she was.

Something about that detail was familiar and tugged at the edges of her memory. Then she remembered how illegal dragon-shifter auctions often required every bidder to follow a strict set of rules, one of which was about the car used to access the event. If everyone drove the same type, it'd be harder to pinpoint anyone who attended the buying and selling of dragon-shifters.

Rather than feeling triumphant at figuring out what was probably happening here, her stomach only churned harder. Because no undercover agent had ever successfully infiltrated one of these events. At least, to her knowledge.

Which meant she would have to find Ethan and try to escape on her own.

And that was going to be near impossible.

Especially since a quick check revealed she had nothing in her pockets. And with no phone or money, escaping and surviving in a desert for long was nearly impossible, especially for someone like her, who'd never even been camping.

Then she noticed a stream of people carrying small, limp forms—a mixture of children and women—and she clenched her fingers into fists. She couldn't simply abandon them. Ethan might even be among them.

So no matter what, she needed to find a way to contact either her sister or MirrorPeak and let them know where she was. Contacting ADDA or DOCS in general was too risky, given the rumors of spies and double agents everywhere.

Prying her eyes from the window, she searched the room. And while there was a landline jack, there was no physical phone.

Which meant she needed to explore other parts of this building.

After getting to the door, she turned the knob and was surprised it moved. However, she released it without tugging and peeked through the old-fashioned keyhole. No one was on the other side, and she made out a narrow hallway, just as dirty and neglected as her room.

The next step was to escape.

The pounding was mostly gone, and she could walk normally, which was a good sign. Plus, the arrivals should keep most people's attention in the vicinity. At least, if she were in charge of something like this, she'd make sure all the staff were on the lookout for cops, ADDA, or the FBI, and not on one random human drugged unconscious.

Luckily for her, someone must've given her too low of a dose.

Okay, Lexi. Time to be brave and see if we can get help. Slowly, she turned the knob again, opened the door a crack, and listened. However, it was the same hum as before, so she opened the door—grateful it didn't squeak —and tiptoed down the short hallway. The building was old, and the wooden floors and walls made her think it was from early last century.

Tucking that bit of knowledge away for later, she reached a sort of living room space, but it was devoid of furniture. Well, everything but an old, dirty lawn chair.

Which was empty.

Since there was no phone, she moved to a small room with a sink that looked to be a kitchen. Despite the age of the building, there was a power outlet over the counter in the room.

And attached to it was a phone.

After checking the hallway again, she went to the phone and tried to unlock it. However, it required a pattern. She tried one of the most obvious—an L-shape down the middle—and it worked. Her elation was short-lived since there were zero bars.

Which explained why someone would leave it lying around with her nearby.

Still, she tucked the phone into her pocket. Because at least now, she had a chance to call someone if she could find some service.

Not wasting time, Lexi found the back door and peered out. The coast was clear, so she exited and went to the edge of the building, leaned against it, and peered around the corner. Fewer people were handing cars over to what looked like some sort of valets. However, she took a minute to watch where one man drove to park the car.

The spot was about a quarter of a mile away from the center of activity.

Lexi was torn. She wanted to confirm Ethan was here and see if she could help him. And yet, her chances against all the criminals here, plus their wealthy bidders who wouldn't want a witness, weren't good. Her best bet would be to steal a car and drive to find a spot that had cell service so she could get help. Because it would take more than her to rescue anyone and escape.

Silently pleading for Ethan to be okay, she quietly walked toward the back of the yard, hiding as best she could from the obvious security cameras—someone wanted everyone to know they were watching—and from the people filing into the large building in the center of what looked like an abandoned town. A ghost town, maybe?

Lexi kept checking, but the phone had zero bars as she walked. She focused on using the buildings to hide her, getting her ever closer to the parked cars. Every step made her realize just how hot it was outside and how dry her mouth was.

Lexi would never take water for granted again.

Once she was as close to the parked vehicles as she could get without being seen, she suddenly had three bars.

Ha! Of course they'd safeguard the cars.

Lexi quickly dialed the number for MirrorPeak's Protector building, one she'd also made Ethan memorize. A male voice picked up and answered after the second ring. "Who is this?"

"Lexi Sakamoto. Listen—I'm in some sort of abandoned town in the desert where I think they're holding an illegal dragon auction. Please send someone here to help. Can you trace this phone?"

After a split second, the voice replied, "I'm already doing that. Tell me everything you've seen, to help us with the rescue."

Even though she wanted to ask questions, Lexi

focused on giving as many details as possible. Because, as soon as someone discovered she was gone, her odds weren't good.

She'd just finished filling in the dragonman with details when something crashed against the back of her head, and pain exploded before the world went black.

Kyle and his two nurses flew a few miles behind the rest of the dragons heading toward Duncan Parrish's property. A scout had gone ahead and confirmed there were a lot of people there, all following rules and patterns they thought were typical of the black-market dragon auctions.

He was wondering if the others in front had arrived yet when he heard screams.

His dragon spoke up. *That must be them.*

Kyle's instinct was to fly faster. However, he'd promised to give the Protectors time to get control of the property and tie up any humans they knocked unconscious.

And yet, every second seemed like an hour. Eventually, there were a series of whistles that signaled it was safe for the medical team to land.

He wasted no time pumping his wings, and soon the small town in the middle of nowhere came into view. The buildings were mostly old and tiny, except for a large one in the center. However, he barely gave them a second glance, searching for the flares marking where he could land.

There. Not far from a lot of parked cars—some of which were motionless on the dirt road out of the place, as if people had been trying to escape—was a cleared section, with a dragon on the ground, standing guard. There were also a few Protectors in human form walking among females and children.

No doubt the ones who'd been about to be sold.

Pushing down his anger, Kyle landed and imagined his wings shrinking into his back, his limbs growing smaller, and his snout returning to his nose and face. Once he was in human form, he quickly tugged on some clothes—for hygiene reasons, as being naked didn't bother him—and walked toward Daniel, who crouched next to a female.

Kyle was about to ask for a status update when he noticed Lexi's still form on the ground.

With a roar, he rushed to her side, knelt down, and checked her pulse. It was there, but faint.

And a quick exam revealed blood on the back of her head, as well as welts around her wrists.

Daniel spoke. "She won't wake up. I think she was hit on the head from behind."

Which meant she might be bleeding into her brain.

Gently cupping her cheek, Kyle wanted to tell her it would be okay, that he could save her right then and there.

But he couldn't. She needed to be scanned and possibly have surgery.

Normally, he'd already be barking orders to prepare the carrying trays used for rescues. It was one of the few times they could legally fly humans—when they needed to be moved to safety and for medical attention.

And yet, as he stroked her overly warm cheek, all he could do was imagine the worst.

Despite the fear roiling around in his belly, he managed to ask, "And what about Ethan?"

Daniel replied, "He was here, but we haven't found him yet. We're looking, though, and won't give up. And I can see you're torn, Kyle. But take her back to Mirror-Peak and get her help. Dr. Alvaro might need you. We'll find Ethan, I vow it."

He finally tore his gaze from Lexi's still form and met his friend's eyes.

His dragon spoke up. *We'd trust Daniel with our life. Let him find Ethan. Right now, Lexi needs more help, or she might die.*

Even though his beast was right, he hesitated. Ethan was his son. It felt wrong abandoning him after just finding him.

Daniel said, "Go with her. None of the Protectors will allow you outside of the medical area here, anyway. We'll find Ethan, no matter what. Trust me, Kyle. I won't abandon your son."

Even a month ago, Kyle might've balked at trusting

others to help him. He'd kept himself apart, and he'd grown distant.

However, in recent weeks, he'd gotten to know his friends and clan better.

So he nodded. "Thank you, Daniel."

Daniel grunted. "Of course. Now, go. Lexi was the only one who needed immediate medical attention. The nurses can handle the rest for now."

With that, Kyle barked orders to ready the carrying basket. And once Lexi was in it, he stayed with her, holding her hand and telling her she'd better pull through or he'd never forgive her.

Kyle paced the private waiting room, waiting for Dr. Alvaro to give him an update.

She'd been in surgery for hours trying to save Lexi, who had a bleed in the brain. And if the dragonwoman couldn't stop it, Lexi wouldn't survive.

While he was grateful that Dr. Alvaro's specialty was neurosurgery—even though she could do routine surgeries too, like any dragon doctor—he still didn't like how she'd banned him from even watching the operation.

His dragon spoke up. *You would distract her. It's hard enough performing brain surgery without having someone staring her down.*

He grunted. *That might be true, but I don't have to like it.*

Before his beast could reply, there was a knock, and the door opened. He expected to see the doctor or one of the nurses, but Ethan rushed in. Joy and relief rushed through him as Kyle dropped down, opened his arms, and caught his son as he jumped into them. "Ethan! You're safe."

The boy hugged him harder.

As Kyle stroked his son's head, he asked, "Are you okay?"

The boy nodded, but didn't say anything. Kyle slowly moved back until he could see Ethan's face. His pupils flashed rapidly, but he wouldn't meet his eyes. "What's wrong?"

"I shouldn't have believed him."

"Who?"

"That man. He said you were my real dad and didn't want me, gave me away, and that you were going to sell me to the dragon hunters."

"Wait, slow down. Tell me everything."

And as Kyle listened to how Ethan's maternal uncle had filled the boy's head with doubts, making him think Kyle really didn't want him, he began to understand why his son had gone with that male.

At the end, Ethan finally met his gaze. "Is it true? Are you my dad? My real dad?"

Even though he rather would've waited to talk about this, Kyle nodded. "Yes. I didn't know you existed,

Ethan, or I would've made sure you knew how to be a dragon-shifter. I promise you that."

"And now? Do you want me now?"

Kyle placed a hand on his son's shoulder, squeezed, and nodded. "Yes, I want you. And not just because you're my son. I love you, Ethan, and I want to help you learn to be a dragon-shifter, to become a grown male, to do all the things you want to do, and to be a family."

Ethan hesitated and then blurted, "And what about Lexi? Will she die?"

He didn't want to lie and struggled with how to answer. "Dr. Alvaro is doing everything she can."

"I don't want her to die."

He pulled his son into another hug. "Neither do I, Ethan. Neither do I."

As he continued to hold his boy, Dr. Alvaro entered the room. Kyle's heart pounded since he couldn't read her expression. But she spoke before he could ask anything. "Lexi pulled through. And provided she wakes up, she should make a full recovery."

Ethan turned. "Will she wake up?"

The female doctor's face softened a little. "I think so, but sometimes we don't know what will happen when someone's hit on the head. The brain is in your head, and sometimes it does what it wants to and we can't predict it."

Ethan's face looked uncertain, so Kyle added, "But we'll visit her as soon as we can and make sure she knows we want her to wake up."

Ethan bobbed his head. "I'll tell her over and over again. She was always so nice to me, and I don't want her to die. Or leave. Can she stay here?"

Kyle smiled. "I hope she stays here. I'll have to convince her as much as I can, once she wakes up."

"When can we see her?" Ethan asked.

Dr. Alvaro answered, "Soon. You two should eat something and then you can visit Lexi." Kyle opened his mouth to protest, but the doctor beat him to it. "Ethan needs something in his belly to help erase the last bits of drugs in his system."

Anger spiked at knowing his son had been drugged. He studied Ethan's face, and he noticed some signs of fatigue he'd overlooked at first. Probably because Kyle hadn't slept in nearly a day himself. "Okay, let's go get some pizza for you and we'll come back and see Lexi."

Kyle stood, took Ethan's hand, and said quietly to Dr. Alvaro, "Thank you."

She inclined her head. "Of course. You've already done me a favor, even if you don't know it."

Before he could ask what that meant, she exited the room.

Ethan tugged on his hand and said, "Let's hurry and get some pizza. I want to see Lexi."

"Just for a little while and then you need to get some sleep."

"But—"

"We can set up a cot in Lexi's room, if you want. But

it's been a long day and you need some rest to feel more awake and like yourself again."

"Okay, I guess."

He resisted smiling at Ethan's petulant tone. "Come on. The sooner we eat, the sooner we can see Lexi."

And as Kyle took care of his son, he hoped one day soon Lexi could be there with them, eating pizza and talking about inner dragons with Ethan.

His dragon spoke up. *We'll let Lexi know as many times as it takes that she needs to wake up and complete our family.*

His dragon's words made him feel a little better. *I'll also tap every favor I have if Lexi needs more medical assistance or a specialist.*

Good. The sooner she's better, the sooner we can claim her.

While Kyle wanted that more than anything, he only hoped Lexi hadn't been scared away from dragon-shifters after her ordeal. He wouldn't blame her, seeing as trying to help Ethan had made her a target of the League.

However, Kyle wouldn't let that hold him back. Lexi was his. He'd ensure his clan would protect her, and he'd make sure she knew it.

Chapter Thirteen

L exi was aware of someone talking to her, although the voices were garbled and unclear.

Her head also hurt, and she struggled to wake up. Bit by bit the voices became defined until she could make out, "This is how you fly when with a group of friends. That way, you can each look out for each other, in case someone pulls a muscle and falls behind."

"But how do you not crash into someone?"

"Lots of practice."

It took her a second, but then she placed the voices: Kyle and Ethan.

Ethan! Hearing the boy motivated Lexi to try harder to open her eyes. It took longer than she liked, but eventually she opened them and blinked against the light and groaned.

Someone gently grabbed her hand. "Lexi, are you awake? Tell me, love. Please."

Kyle. Her eyes finally focused on the large dragonman above her. His pupils flashed, and she noticed the stubble on his jaw. "You look like hell."

He chuckled. "Not the first thing I expected you to say, but I'm glad to hear it." His voice dropped a fraction. "You scared me, Lexi. You scared the both of us."

Before she could reply, Ethan's head popped into her field of vision. "Lexi, are you okay? Did you hear me tell you to wake up?"

She smiled, wishing she was strong enough to sit up and hug Ethan. Her voice was still crackly as she replied, "I don't remember, but I'm sure it made the difference. I'm glad you're okay."

Ethan patted her shoulder. "You helped them find us. You were brave and smart and I'm sorry they hurt you."

She frowned and glanced at Kyle, and he answered, "Your information helped them form a better plan, according to Rio and Axel." He cupped her cheek and caressed her skin with his thumb. "I'm glad you're here with us now, love. We both are."

It was the second time he'd used the endearment. Part of her yearned to ask what it meant, secretly hoping he still wanted her as his mate. But her head buzzed a little, and she wasn't sure she could handle a complex or serious conversation right now.

Although she hoped they could talk about it later because during her escape attempt, she'd realized how much she yearned to return to Kyle, run into his arms, and never leave his or Ethan's side again.

For now, she murmured, "Water and then tell me everything."

Kyle frowned as he reached for the nearby cup. "You should wait until you're stronger before we go over all that." He lifted her head and placed the cup at her lips. "Here, drink this. Slowly."

After she drank a little water and sighed with relief, she said, "Please, tell me. Is everyone okay?"

Once she settled back on her pillow, he said, "Yes. We rescued all the dragon-shifters and most of the attendees were handed over to ADDA. No one knows what will happen to them—no doubt some will make deals and give information—but I doubt they'll use that location again for any sort of illegal activity."

Ethan moved closer to Kyle. "I don't want them to take me again."

"They won't. I'll protect you. The entire clan will. I vow it, Ethan."

As the boy snuggled into his father's side, Lexi's heart warmed. More than ever, she wanted that future.

However, before she accidentally blurted that, Dr. Alvaro came in, shooed Kyle and Ethan out, and then asked her a series of questions. By the end, the doctor told her it would take some time to recover. And even though she yearned to talk more with Kyle and Ethan, her eyelids drooped and Lexi fell fast asleep.

The next time she woke up, her sister sat in a chair next to her bed, typing something on a laptop. Lexi blinked. "Jennifer?"

Her sister placed the computer on the side table, stood, and took her hand. "Lexi! Thank goodness. I would hug you, but I don't want to hurt you."

"Not that I don't love seeing you, but why are you here?"

Her sister arched a dark eyebrow. "You were drugged, kidnapped, and bashed over the head. Of course I came to see you."

As she studied her sister's face, she could tell Jennifer was hiding something. "What is it, Jen? It's not like you to beat around the bush."

Her sister sighed. "It's not good news."

Ignoring her pounding heart, she said, "Just tell me."

"Well, you've become a major target of the League now, Lexi. They even have your picture posted all over the dark web, with an offer of a small reward for your capture."

"What? Why?"

"You foiled the plans of a rather powerful alleged ally of the League, and he doesn't like it. And so now your future will be one of two options—enter Witness Protection or stay with a dragon clan who can watch over you."

Even though she knew the answer, she couldn't help but blurt, "And my job with DOCS?"

Her sister shook her head. "I'm sorry, but the best they'll let you do is help with clans in the area, if you decide to stay with a dragon clan."

Lexi wanted to stay with Kyle more than anything. But she didn't want him to feel obligated. Because the only way humans were usually allowed to stay on a dragon clan was to mate a dragon-shifter.

And yet, the thought of leaving him and never seeing him or Ethan again made her heart squeeze. Would he want her, even if she didn't mention she had to make the choice?

Sitting on the side of her bed, Jennifer said, "I haven't told Kyle about your options."

"Please, don't."

Her sister leaned over and gave her a one-armed hug. "I won't. But for what it's worth, I think the dragon doctor cares for you, Lexi, if not loves you. He's been a complete, overprotective bear—or, er, dragon, I guess—since I arrived. I had to get the clan leader to come and force him out so I could spend some time with you." Her voice softened. "Do you feel the same way about him? The human named Jenny Torres here seems to think so, but I want to hear it from you. No matter your answer, I'll fight to keep you safe and stay in your life, I promise."

As she studied her older sister's face, her eyes heated with tears. Jennifer had always looked out for her and had given up so much when they'd been younger to try and make Lexi feel less alone once their mother had left.

And she was doing it again, without a thought. "You can't give up your job, Jen. You love it."

Her sister waved a hand in dismissal. "Tell me your answer, and we'll figure the rest out. Because if you want to mate Kyle, then me keeping my job and being in your life will be easier than you think."

"I don't want him to feel like he has to."

Jennifer rolled her eyes. "If that dragonman doesn't love you, then I'll shave my head. At least talk to him. Maybe don't mention the two choices until after you see how he feels."

She sighed. "I guess. I never thought I'd be that woman, the one who falls so easily. And yet..."

"Well, dragonmen have their charms, for sure. Especially if you're his true mate. Are you?"

Needing to unload, she told her sister everything—about being Kyle's true mate, his son, and what she'd seen at the place in the desert. By the end, her sister had one question. "Do you love him then?"

Lexi rubbed her forehead. "I think so. I mean, waking up in that abandoned building in the desert, unsure if I was going to die or not, I kept thinking of Kyle and Ethan. Of how I wished I could see them again and finally have a family of my own."

Her sister took her hand and squeezed. "Sometimes these things happen fast. A long relationship before a mating doesn't make a difference. Just look at me."

"I'm sorry, Jen. I forgot all about him."

"I was young and naïve. But having met Kyle, you're both grown-ass adults, and he clearly knows what he wants. And that's you and Ethan."

"I guess that means I have to talk with him, huh?"

"Yep. But not before you tell me some more about him. Oh, and I need to call the doctor soon. I promised I would once you woke up again."

And as Lexi talked with her sister, her doubts melted away one by one. She loved Kyle and Ethan, and she wanted to stay with MirrorPeak. She might not be able to keep her job with DOCS, but that didn't mean she couldn't do other things to help humans and dragon-shifters get along, or even help the children find forever families.

By the time her sister left and Dr. Alvaro arrived, Lexi was confident about her next steps. However, she wanted to be out of this hospital bed and well again before she took them.

Chapter Fourteen

Kyle had spent the last three weeks settling Ethan into his home and life, visiting Lexi whenever he could, and helping out Dr. Alvaro as much as she'd allow at the clinic.

And while his life was almost the busiest it'd been in a long time, he didn't mind.

Especially since Lexi had finally been discharged from the clinic and her mandatory physical therapy rehab, and would be coming to stay with him.

He still couldn't believe she was going to stay on MirrorPeak. About a week after the incident in the desert, she'd asked if he still wanted to date and get to know her. If he might still want to claim her.

Man and beast hadn't hesitated and had said yes.

It'd taken another week for him to wheedle out that she had to make a choice about her future, and soon. Either with him and MirrorPeak, or whisked away to some unknown location, to live her life under a false name.

He hadn't gone as far as to say he loved her—yet, as he was waiting for a better time—but he'd asked her to mate him. And she'd said yes.

Technically, they were already mates. Rio had thought it best to get the paperwork side of things done. And yet, they'd lived apart since Lexi had stayed at the clinic.

But she was coming home today. Not only that, Ethan was staying with his Aunt Rita for a bit, to allow the frenzy.

If Lexi was ready.

His dragon spoke up. *We've almost kissed her several times this week. I hope she's ready.*

If not, then we'll be patient. It's a big step for her. For all of us.

Kyle had already talked with Ethan about a future sibling. The boy had been reluctant at first, and Kyle couldn't blame him for it. However, he'd gone out of his way to assure his son that he'd be there, wouldn't give him away, and that Ethan would be an amazing big brother.

Mating Lexi had helped Ethan accept the idea. The boy already loved Lexi, and she was doing her best to be a good stepmom. Well, as best as she could over the last weeks.

Before he could think of what to do if Lexi wasn't ready, the doorbell rang.

His beast spoke up. *That's her.*

While he'd intended to pick her up from the clinic, Jenny Torres had said no. She wanted to fully prepare Lexi for what was in store, as well as answer any of her lingering questions.

In the end, he'd agreed that was a good idea. Humans who didn't know about the frenzy sometimes became terrified.

The doorbell rang. He rushed to the door, opened it, and promptly stopped breathing.

Lexi stood there in a simple sundress, one that showed off her tan shoulders and arms. She had a pretty clip in her short hair, and a simple chain around her neck. Dangling from the chain was the pendant he'd given her as a mating present—a dragon with its wings spread and its eye a dark emerald.

She was beautiful, so beautiful, and he had to count to three, slowly, to keep his cock from reacting.

She smiled at him. "Can I come in?"

Moving aside, he gestured, and she entered the house before he shut the door. "Where's Jenny?"

"She walked me most of the way, but I wanted to show up alone."

She ran her fingers along the back of the sofa, stopped at the end, and turned around.

Not wanting her to feel pressured, Kyle stopped a few feet from her and resisted touching her face. "If you have any more questions, feel free to ask. But just know that we can wait as long as you need."

She tilted her head. "Do you want to wait?"

"No!" He cleared his throat. "No. But at the end of it, we'll have a child on the way. Between mating me, moving to MirrorPeak, and becoming Ethan's stepmom, that's a lot to adjust to. I don't want you to run screaming for the hills."

"Well, we *are* on top of a mountain. So I would have to run screaming down the hill."

His lips twitched as he took a step closer. "I don't want you screaming because of anything, unless it's from pleasure."

Lexi closed the gap between them and placed a hand on his chest, over his T-shirt. Each stroke of her fingers sent heat through his body, straight to his cock.

His dragon spoke up. *She wants us. Stop dawdling.*

Not yet. Give me some time.

His beast sniffed. *A little, but not too long.*

Reaching a hand over, he cupped her cheek. Lexi leaned into his touch and stepped closer, until they were nearly chest-to-chest. He whispered, "Tell me what you want, love. I'm yours to command."

Her fingers stilled, ran up, and moved to the back of his neck. As she played with his hair, she murmured, "I want you to kiss me, Kyle. I've thought of nothing else since Dr. Alvaro said I would be discharged today."

He moved his hand to the small of her back and pulled her flush against him. At the feel of her warm, soft body, he growled. "Tell me you're sure, Lexi.

Because once I do, you either have to knee me in the balls and flee, or go through the frenzy."

She leaned more against him, and he could feel the hard points of her nipples against his chest. His dragon flashed images of suckling her tight little buds, making her moan and beg for more.

"Kiss me, Kyle. I'm ready."

After tracing her cheek with his finger, he cupped her head, leaned down, and whispered, "Then it's time to claim my mate for real."

As soon as his lips touched hers, need flooded his body and his dragon roared. *She's ours to claim. Ours. Kiss her, fuck her, claim her over and over again until she carries our scent and our young.*

Kyle did his best to tamp down his dragon's demands and needs as he kissed his female properly for the first time. Brushing his lips over hers, she moaned and opened. His tongue slipped inside her mouth, and he held her closer against him as he licked and explored and took time to nibble first her bottom lip and then the top one.

Her hands roamed his back, and he grabbed her ass with his free one, rocking her against his now stone-like cock. She squirmed deliberately, which only made him take the kiss deeper.

The longer he kissed her, the louder his dragon roared inside his head until he finally said, *Either fuck her first, now, or I'll take control.*

Remember our bargain, dragon.

You're taking too long. So act, or I'll claim her.

Kyle finally broke the kiss, rested his forehead against Lexi's, and murmured, "I could kiss you for days and never get enough."

"But your dragon is impatient?" she finished for him.

"Yes." He kissed her briefly. "So take off your clothes because I want to see your beautiful body before I claim you."

Lexi stepped back, toyed with the hem of her dress, and Kyle's cock pounded with need as he waited to see what his female would do next.

Lexi's heart thudded inside her chest as she watched Kyle's pupils flash from slits to round and back again, faster than she'd ever seen before.

His dragon was impatient.

While ideally she'd like her first time with Kyle to be slow and full of heat and laughter, her mate wasn't human but a dragon-shifter.

Mate. She still couldn't believe it.

However, Kyle growled, and Lexi knew she had to hurry if she wanted her first time to be with his human half in charge.

So she tugged her dress over her head and kicked off her sandals. She'd been prepared and hadn't worn any underwear or a bra. She was naked.

For a split second, she wondered if Kyle would like

what he saw. But as her dragonman's gaze roamed her body, his eyes flashing with heat and approval, her skin heated and more wetness rushed between her thighs.

While she knew his dragon would take control later, for now, she was grateful to have the human half ease her into all of this.

Kyle met her eyes again and tore off his own shirt and shorts. When he was finally naked, her eyes shot to his long, hard cock jutting from his body. He stroked his dick a few times as he prowled toward her.

Yes, prowled seemed the right word.

Once he reached her, he released himself, scooped her up, and Lexi squeaked as her arms wrapped around his neck. "I hope we're not going to do this on the kitchen counter for the first time."

He snorted, headed for the stairs, and nuzzled her cheek. "For a frenzy, a bed is best. You'll get sore and tired, and I don't want to add to that."

She caressed his cheek, his jaw, the bridge of his nose. "Oh, don't rule out sex in other places after the frenzy. But given what Jenny said, a bed will help."

The woman had described the frenzy as amazing yet exhausting, and by the end, she'd be sore.

But she'd never, ever forget it.

And given Jenny's fond smile, Lexi had only looked forward to it herself.

Kyle reached his bed, laid her down, and put a hand to either side of her hips. "Ready, love?" He moved a hand between her legs and stroked, making Lexi moan. "I think you are."

Spreading her thighs, she reached up and pulled his face closer. "We can tease and take it slow later. For now, claim me, Kyle. I'm ready to be your mate for real."

With that, he took her lips in a fierce kiss as he laid on top of her. Wrapping her legs around his hips, she rubbed against him, loving how he sucked in a breath before taking the kiss even deeper.

One hand played between her legs, stroking slowly but never quite touching her clit. She arched, wanting him to touch her there, but he pulled away.

She growled. "I thought we had to do this quickly, so why are you being so slow?"

With a chuckle, he kissed her nose, sat back on his heels, and ran his cock through her center. Up, down, but never pushing inside. "My dragon will only be thinking of fucking and nothing else. And since my semen will make you orgasm, he'll still preen. I want you nice and wet for me, Lexi. It'll make this easier for you."

As he continued to tease her opening, Lexi arched up so that he touched her clit, and pleasure flared.

She'd never felt this turned on so quickly in her life before.

Kyle finally positioned his dick at her entrance, and inch by inch, slid inside her. Once he finally was in to the hilt, she moaned. He was hard and thick, and it was almost too much.

Then he rubbed her clit with his fingers in firm, slow

strokes as he moved his hips, and she forgot about everything but the building sensation—heat and pleasure and a fullness she'd never felt before.

He growled as he picked up his pace. "Fuck, you're so tight and wet and perfect, love."

His words only made her hotter, and she was close, so close.

His eyes never left hers, his pupils flashing. His expression was a mixture of desire, lust, and... tenderness.

Maybe even love.

Before she could think too hard on that, he lightly pinched her clit. Lights exploded in front of her eyes as ecstasy shot through her body, in wave after wave, made more intense by Kyle still moving inside her.

Just as she started to come down from her high, he stilled and growled. And as he came, another orgasm washed over her.

By the time her spasms finally eased, Kyle lay heavy on top of her, and she ran her hands down his slightly damp back. The feel of his weight and heat, and being surrounded by his scent, made her simultaneously feel safe and eager for more.

She kissed the side of his neck and said, "I'm ready for your dragon, Kyle."

He grunted, raised his head, and kissed her slowly. When he pulled away, his pupils remained slitted. "Mine. Time to claim what's mine."

And Lexi waited to see what his dragon half would do.

Kyle was still trying to gather the energy to kiss and reassure Lexi when she said, "I'm ready for your dragon, Kyle."

His inner beast roared. *My turn. I want to claim our female. I've waited long enough.*

Just remember, after once, you let her rest. Lexi's human and not used to this.

I know. Now, give me my turn.

He retreated inside his mind to let his dragon take over. He lifted their head and growled. "Mine. Time to claim what's mine."

And Lexi merely smiled. "Then take me."

With another growl, his beast moved them upright, flipped Lexi on her belly, and raised her hips. Kyle hadn't been lying when he said the dragon half would be straight to the point as his beast positioned their already hard-again cock and thrust inside Lexi.

She moaned, arched her back, and his beast took a hold of her hips and moved, increasing his pace. Some dragon halves would merely do that, focused on chasing their orgasm and trying to get their true mate pregnant.

However, as Lexi moved her hips to meet them, his dragon reached a hand around and fondled her clit. After a few more pumps, she cried out, gripping and releasing their dick. Soon his dragon stilled and released inside her, triggering another orgasm.

On and on it went, more intense than with anyone in the past, and both man and beast knew they'd never tire of their female. Ever.

As their breathing calmed, Kyle said to his dragon, *Let me back in charge. She needs a rest and probably some comfort.*

Human stuff is your job. But don't make me wait too long. I want to claim her, again and again, until she carries our child.

I won't. Now, let me take care of her.

Bit by bit, his dragon retreated, allowing Kyle to take control of their mind again. He rolled to the side, brought Lexi with them, and hugged her close. "I'm back."

He felt her smile against his chest. "Your dragon doesn't mess around."

As he stroked her hip, he chuckled. "I did warn you."

She looked up to meet his gaze. "Well, the variety means our sex life will never be boring."

His dragon sniffed. *Never.*

Kyle chuckled and shared his dragon's thoughts, and Lexi stroked his chest as she said, "I'm glad I asked if you still wanted to mate me."

He hugged her tighter. "Why you ever doubted it, I'll never understand."

"Well, it was fast. Much faster than I ever thought it could happen, especially..."

"Especially what?"

She bit her lip and stared at his chest. He continued to stroke her skin, not liking how she hesitated.

His beast spoke up. *Just tell her our feelings and maybe she won't hold back. I don't want her to think we don't truly want her.*

Kyle moved his hand to under her chin and gently made her look at him again. After pressing his lips to hers, he said, "I love you, Lexi Sakamoto. And if it takes the rest of my life to convince you I mean it and am glad you decided to mate me, I'll do it."

She searched his gaze. "You love me?"

Cupping her cheek, he nodded. "I do. Not only because you're kind and funny and brave, but you see me, the real me, and aren't afraid to call me out. As a clan doctor, it's sometimes hard for other clan members to speak up. Not because I'd be mad—well, most of the time, since no one enjoys being wrong—but it's a fine line. However, you pointed out how being isolated hurt everyone and helped no one, and you were right." He laid his forehead against hers. "You knew what I needed, even if I didn't want to admit it. You know me, Lexi. You see me. And you already love Ethan as your own. So yes, I love you. And I look forward to seeing what our future holds."

She smiled, kissed him, and when she finally broke it, she said, "I love you, too, Kyle Baker. You're smart, and caring, and more fun than you originally let on." He raised his brows, and she laughed. "It's true. You tease and get overly competitive over horseshoes, and are already moving mountains for your son. And even when I hated being a burden when I was recovering, you went above and beyond to take care of me."

"You were never a burden, love."

She placed a finger over his lips. "I was. But let me finish. Despite all of that, and learning to be a parent, I know you contacted the other clan doctors and clan leaders so that I can help with any of their orphan candidates as a type of mediator. You made sure I didn't have to give up my life completely. For all that, and so much more, I love you."

He took her lips in a deep kiss, slow and possessive, to let her know without words how much he loved her.

And when he finally pulled away, she yawned, and Kyle settled back and held her close. "Sleep, love. My dragon only has so much patience, and we have a lot of days ahead of us before the frenzy finishes."

Snuggling into his side, she said, "I love you, Kyle. Both sides of you."

His inner dragon stood tall as Kyle replied, "I love you, too. We both do. Now, sleep and dream of our future."

As her breathing slowed and she slipped into slumber, Kyle held his female close and dreamed of a life with his mate, his son, and their baby. One of love and friendship, as far as possible from the self-imposed isolation he'd lived for far too long.

Epilogue

A Little Over Two Years Later

Lexi held her baby daughter, Mika, against her hip as she watched Kyle and Ethan play a game of horseshoes. During the summer, her family had biweekly get-togethers with the Torres family, and this week had been her and Kyle's time to host.

As Mika leaned to one side, wanting down, Lexi debated putting her on the ground when Jenny came up with her son, Camden, next to her. Her daughter stretched toward the little boy. "Down!"

Once Lexi had placed her daughter down, she teetered a second before waddling over to Camden. He held out a stuffed dragon. Mika squealed, took it, and held it close. Her daughter had a penchant for stuffed dragons, and this one was bright pink with sparkly eyes.

Jenny smiled. "Camden saw it and wanted to get it for Mika. Who knows, maybe they'll end up being true mates one day."

She snorted. "Let's not get ahead of ourselves."

Rubbing her ever-growing belly, Jenny looked wistfully at her son. "I hope he loves his sibling as much."

She hugged her friend. "Don't be silly. There's a bigger gap between Ethan and Mika, and Ethan is the most loving and overprotective brother ever."

As if he'd heard her, Ethan ran over and skidded to a halt. His pupils flashed as he said, "I won! Even with Dad trying to cheat, I won!"

Kyle had reached them and sighed. "You've become really skilled at the game, son. Maybe I'm getting too old."

Ethan shook his head. "Aunt Rita can still beat me. You just suck at the game."

Lexi bit back a smile at Kyle's affronted face. "Well, your father can still beat you in a swimming contest. So we each have our strengths."

Kyle moved to her side, wrapped an arm around her waist, and kissed her forehead. "Have I mentioned how much I love you lately?"

Ethan scrunched his nose. "If you're getting kissy, I'm leaving. Uncle Daniel said I could play him next."

Even though Ethan and Mika were unrelated to

Daniel and Jenny by blood, they were their aunt and uncle in every other way.

Jenny smiled. "I'll join you."

Ethan sighed. "Uncle Daniel isn't going to like that."

"Well, Cam will help me, so Daniel will have a fighting chance." She put out her hand to her son, and he took it just as Kyle scooped up their daughter.

Jenny waved goodbye as Kyle wrapped his free arm around Lexi's shoulders. She laid her head against her mate, traced her daughter's cheek, and murmured, "Today is nearly perfect."

"Nearly? If you mean your sister, she'll be here next week."

Her sister had ended up mating a dragonman from a different clan, but still visited when she could. "I know. But I'm also talking about Ashley Swift. She's been really busy lately, but she always makes things fun with me and Jenny."

However, Ashley's mate was busy formalizing the alliances between all the Tahoe dragon clans. Even if the country as a whole had a long way to go, things were progressing in her part of the world.

She'd even helped plan the first human-dragon summer camp. She might not formally work for DOCS, but they hired her as a consultant sometimes, so she still helped the dragon orphans when she could.

He nuzzled her neck and murmured, "Aunt Rita is taking the children tonight for a sleepover, so I can help you have fun."

His words sent a rush of heat through her body. "Hmm, could you?"

He lightly swatted her butt. "For that, I'm going to draw it out and maybe make you beg."

"Good."

His pupils flashed rapidly. However, before he could say anything else, Mika held up her stuffed dragon. "Fly, Daddy! Fly!"

After Kyle kissed her, he played with their daughter, holding her with her stomach facing the ground so she could pretend to fly.

Watching the formally so-serious doctor utter sound effects and make their daughter laugh made her heart warm.

She never would've guessed that some dragonman ignoring her emails and riling her temper would've ended up being her happy ending. But she wouldn't have it any other way.

Author's Note

I hope you liked Kyle and Lexi's story! I'm not sure I'll write another novella with an older kid again, though. Having three "main characters" in 36,000 words, and trying to make them fleshed out and relatable, is really hard! Especially for an established series like this one, where there are certain expectations for how they play out.

I *think* the next story will be about Eli, the injured dragonman that nearly died in this story. I want to say I know his true mate, but I'm not going to pigeon-hole myself into anything right now! Hopefully the next Tahoe story will be out in 2026. As of writing this, I'm currently writing Stonefire Dragons #17 and then will write a book in the Dark Lords of London series. So I have a few full-length books to do first.

And a little side note, but before writing this story I re-read all of my Tahoe books and took notes. Normally, I do this when I proof my audiobooks. However, this series isn't in audio (yet...someday) and I'd forgotten a lot. One of the biggest things was I introduced Jennifer

Sakamoto back in *The Dragon's Bidder* but forgot she existed when I wrote *The Dragon's Find* (Daniel and Jenny's story). I ended up with two Jennifers...so I made a joke about it, lol. These things happen when I have over 400 characters in my greater dragon-shifter universe!

And now I have some people to thank for getting this out into the world:

- To all my beta readers—Sabrina , Iliana, Amy, and Ashley you do an amazing job at finding those lingering typos and minor inconsistencies.

And as always, a huge thank you to you, the reader, for either enjoying my dragons for the first time, or for following me from my longer books to this series. Writing is the best job in the world and it's your support that makes it so I can keep doing it.

Until next time, happy reading!

Cheers,
Jessie

Vampire's Modern Bride

Dark Lords of London #1

An enemies-to-lovers, fated mates, fish-out-of-water romance with vampires, fae witches, shifters, and a dash of time travel magic...

Blackmailed by her father into marrying a ruthless vampire mob boss, Yesenia Vale somehow makes it down the aisle to the male who only wants to use her as a broodmare. After all, she's a fae witch without magic, an outcast, and marrying the bastard is the only way to ensure her brother and sister remain safe from his clutches. However, as soon as the groom slides his ring on her finger, she wishes she could be anywhere else, to have a future of her choosing. In the next moment, the world blacks out. And when she wakes up, she's no longer in twenty-first century Boston but rather in late-nineteenth-century London, blooding a vampire she's never seen before.

Leopold Yates is one of the three Dark Lords of London, ruling over the vampires in the city and doing his best to keep his alliance with the fae witches and shifters to avoid a repeat of their bloody past. Part of how he does it is by remaining in his stronger frozen state, never wanting to find his fated bride. But when a mysterious, half-dressed fae witch shows up in his gaming hell, unconscious, he goes to help her, but touching her skin instantly makes his heart beat again. Even if he hates her for making him weak, he needs to keep her close until he claims her with his fangs and cock. If not, he'll eventually lose his mind and go mad.

Both have something the other needs, and so they strike a bargain. Leo will help Yesenia find a way to contact her family in the future, and she will let him claim her once to stave off madness. But what starts as a business deal ends up morphing into something more. Will they find a way to be together in the past? Or will Leo have to let Yesenia go back to the future to protect her family and lose her forever?

Note: This is a spicy/steamy time-travel romance complete with a grumpy vampire leader, an outcast fae witch with a secret, plenty of spice, and a clash of past versus future views. This story is most definitely not fade to black (ahem, you'll learn what touching a fae witch's pointed ears will do...).

Vampire's Modern Bride is available in paperback.

About the Author

Jessie Donovan has sold over half a million books, has given away hundreds of thousands more to readers for free, and has even hit the *NY Times* and *USA Today* bestseller lists. She is best known for her dragon-shifter series, but also writes about magic users, aliens, and even has a crazy romantic comedy series set in Scotland. When not reading a book, attempting to tame her yard, or traipsing around some foreign country on a shoestring, she can often be found interacting with her readers on Facebook. She lives near Seattle, where, yes, it rains a lot but it also makes everything green.

Visit her website at: www.JessieDonovan.com